THE JOURNEY

THE JOURNEY

Nu D'Guymon

Sun Rose Press

The Journey

Copyright 2015 by Nu D'Guymon

Cover art and layout by Rogue-Art.com

Co-edited by Judith Guymon

Published in the United States by Sun Rose Press

ISBN 978-0-9970261-1-5

Other books by this author

The Book of Zen (Essays)

Published by Nha Xuat Ban Ton Giao, VN 2004

Acknowledgments

Many thanks to all the people who have helped fuel this dream, who have believed in me when I didn't.

And special thanks to my husband David for your unconditional support.

To my Mother

Table of contents

The Private Garden

Jade loves her work but hates her coworkers.

Everybody at her work travels, except Jade. Long, short and in-between trips, they talk about the last exotic destination, looking forward to the next one at the coffee machine gossip center.

There are people whom traveling gives them wings. New experiences fully lived and integrated radiate through their relaxed views and complaisant demeanor.

And people who are merely spectators wherever they live or go, camera ready. Her co-workers.

They flaunt the proof of their happiness on the *Hollywoodish* state of social media, with ape like grins similar to the chemically induced euphoria in addicts; what could be a wondrous experience is reduced to a two dimensional piece of vanity in a substitute world where the ancient art of shoeshine comes back to life. It's a skill elevated to an art form. Dust off unsightly moments of one's life and coat it with a veneer of success and accomplishment to establish one's self-worth. To Jade, a person's basis for self-worth unveils the true identity of that person.

Everybody at her work travels, except Jade. She hides it well, her dirty little secret, because not buying into consumerism is a sin.

Jade finishes the sandwich and tucks her lunch bag under the desk. She stretches and heads toward the washroom on the opposite aisle of the floor. Her after lunch routine: brush her teeth, check her makeup, and squeeze in a short walk. A brief moment away from the screen and clients is a smart way of embracing work. At the turn of the hallway into the rotunda she hears the click clack of high heels on the marble floor before seeing a skinny blond approach on stilettos. It's too late to retreat because Hotshot has seen her.

Jade summons a smile: "Hi."

"Hello Jade!" and "Nice dress."

"Thank you. Not as pretty as yours."

"Oh, this? I like suits in dusty pink. Edgy professional."

"It sure is."

The blond flips her hair and says casually," Last week was a big win for me."

"You're great, of course you would win", Jade said.

Hotshot smiles: "But I think I've had enough with work for now. I'm going to shop for a new wetsuit. We're going scuba diving in Bora Bora next week."

"How nice! You're going to have a great time." *Not really. You don't speak French. You can't even venture out of the prop of a resort scene.*

"Planning vacations yet? Where are you going?"

To my back yard for a rain bath au naturel. "Not yet," Jade answers out loud. *I hope the volcanoes erupt while you're on the beach.*

Hotshot smirks and looks at Jade, with an expression in her eyes that Jade interprets as a pity look for her insipid life.

A life bound to be frugal not by choice, but by necessity and prudence. She has learned that from the volte-face of the family fortune and her divorce.

"Bye". The blond walks away leaving Jade to her routine and her thoughts.

After the divorce, barely settled in the new old house, its roof needed repair. Good price comes with a catch, of course. Unexpected dental work that insurance wouldn't cover. Chips demand crowns and root canals demand immediate attention, resulting in too many unglamorous hits on her timid bank account. The extra cash she carefully puts aside for 'in case' meets in case, so her thirtieth birthday went by clandestinely two days ago.

Jade goes back to work but her mind drifts away from the oppressive office and her heart aches for the place where she can contemplate her thoughts, be still with time, be one with nothingness, where Happiness does not have a form, nor a name. It simply is. Her private garden.

After the infinitely long cubicle day, and after stripping off the uniform of banality into her bright kimono, she curls up in the butterfly garden chair, sipping wine, listening to the day go down with retreating light steps, while the gossiping birds, hidden in the leaves of the apple trees, add joyful notes to the darkened shades of the crepuscule.

The study of Jade's small house has a large sliding glass door that opens into a well-fenced patch of lawn and flower parterres, with a small elevation at the far end.

On that miniature hill, a few apple trees lend their cool shade to Furret her lazy cat in Summer time, grape vines crawl along the fence lace up a wooden pergola, and a sweet Asian pear tree spreads its branches protecting the tall bluestem grass at its foot from inquisitive sunrays.

A path snakes its way from the back patio up the hill, between the jasmine bushes whose blossoms perfume the sinuous path night after night. Sitting on the patio outside the study, she can see the immense sky over the dark green pines in the neighborhood.

In this place wounds mend themselves with the velvet touch of wormwood leaves and the discreet scent of heathers. Aching wants drown themselves in the still water of the nearby birdbath, fear and worries lose their edges along the overflowing creeping thymes. Here, it feels right to be lazy, to be simplistic, to be nobody in the vast world. A dot under the immense sky, staring in awe at the ever changing clouds like looking at the first morning.

Wine even tastes better in the back yard. Free of artificial chemicals lurking in the house, the aroma of grapes comes alive enveloping every sip.

Grass talks and tells her its stories in the silent notes of the wind while hummingbirds flutter away her headache. And time forgets to count.

The last sip of wine empties the glass as the stars wink their bright eyes to the darkening sky. Velvety fingers of shadows caress the farther corners of the garden as the soft dark veil of night slowly wraps Jade in its embrace. Time to bring peace inside.

If only peace could be easily strung around. The morning will see her happy getting ready for work, then again stiffed up at work in the presence of others.

No. Not today. Today she is going to forget the dictatorship of survival, end the debate with reason and celebrate the sun, the moon, imprudence, life.

She longs to discover the mystery of kindness, and its much more mysterious counter-part. To understand the reason sufferings cling to each and every molecule of existence, or to come to terms with the randomness of it all. Any answer will be better than the limbo state of doubt.

Light rushes in from the window as the sun takes the relay from its electric counterfeit. The natural light makes her new grass green tunic hemmed with cotton lace look a tad older, hung loosely over tight algae green Capri pants.

Shiny shoulder length brown hair behaves in a plastic clip at her nape, but the rebellious wisp, as always, falls on the left cheek, accentuates the symmetry of the oval face. Jade has large brown eyes that look but never seem to focus, nonetheless expert at divulging all of the feelings and thoughts that she carefully keeps to herself, *talking eyes*. Right now those eyes are running through the packing list, squinting at their owner's handwriting.

Laptop, the extension of her brain and personal memory device, can't be left home. But she decides not to cram the camera into the handbag, her senses will do fine at keeping the memories intact.

Jade's small frame looks ridiculously disproportionate to the large suitcases belly up on the floor. She continues to throw her favorite clothes in her favorite suitcase, more willing to save time than space, a surfer profiting on the wave of will, before its strength dies down in the depth of the lethargic ocean.

Cosmetics, the ultimate weapon, protection from looking too organic in a cellophane world. Shoes, an affair with too many breakups in vain. Finally, the two suitcases are fat with expectations of home away from home.

Click.

End of hesitation.

Click.

End of reticence. Ready to leave the loving arms of a home and the comfort of routine for the adventures and weathers of the open road. A glowing smile parts her natural colored lips, the excitement of the journey despite delay reaches its home. Her train departs in three hours. The neighbor Laurie will feed Furret and keep an eye on the house.

Iacta alea est. Yes, the die is cast.

Jade opens the back door. Her eyes linger on the patio, the hill, the tall grass, the succulent apples and pears that drag down the branches. She holds back a sigh, for this will be a very long good bye.

The City of Love

The electrically charged atmosphere breathed out excitement. Anticipation of joy twinkled in every pair of eyes. Eager faces of singles stood out among the more composed expressions of the married couples'. Some looked genuinely relaxed and happy, some wore happiness like a mask, because the pinched lips, dropped corners of the mouth and empty look in the eyes betrayed the smile, a fresh coat of paint couldn't quite hide the worm-eaten wood underneath.

Mask on. For going about this town without a partner was a sign of failure: You're not loved! Mask on. You're not supposed to be unhappily married, for hurt should not be shown, misery was not welcomed. Suffering was inappropriate because it would embarrass the onlookers, the truth on display was disconcerting. The bruised egos of the unhappily married went undercover.

When pain had dimensions, every breath took an effort. Living made no sense when it was shadowed by hurt. She was duped. Love was not wonderful. Merely a disease with self-inflicted pain.

Jade wandered into a café among the numerous shops that bordered the cobblestone streets of the ancient city.

The ruins people came to see in this town were the reminder of the transient phenomenon of time. Every worn, eroded rock had witnessed the rise and fall of many empires, many dreams, and much greed. They had seen tears of lovers, hope that did not outlive time, and lives that had left imprints.

The sun has started its trajectory home, lending a magnificent splendor to the remains of the past. The tragic contrast of golden lights on the grayish corpse of a dead city was fascinating to watch. Enthralling and yet repugnant. Like past loves.

Under the scrutinizing light of reality, past love unveiled its face: an extinct need prolonged by egos. All was exposed by Time, the Great Conqueror.

Sitting at the table on the terrace of this no-name cafe, looking at the faceless passing crowd, in the shadow of the past, Jade asked herself why she had to make this stop. Love was overrated.

Her eyes swept the crowd, not looking, not seeing, not expecting, when they fell upon a lady in a long white dress. The white, restful and attractive, detached itself in the ocean of vibrant summer colors on clothes and merchandise all around. A colorless haven.

The lady in the long white dress, tea cup in hand, came and sat by Jade. Jade looked up, a little surprised, a little annoyed, then looked away, drowned in her thoughts, wrapped up in the lonely world of unexpressed anger and frustration. They sipped their teas in the uneasy silence filled with tumultuous thoughts, in this afternoon, in a city just too familiar to Jade, like the companionship of doubt.

The eternal battle, *I put more of my heart into Us and you put less. I care and you don't* ... her stream of voiceless rambling was interrupted.

The conversation began somewhat like this:

"Hello. May I? Are you by yourself?" The Lady-in-White started. Jade was surprised, not by the question, but by the strange softness of her voice.

"I am. Aren't we all? Are you not?"

The soft voice continued: "I do seem to be by myself, but all the pain and joy I have witnessed shadow me; so to answer that question, no, I'm not by myself." As strange as the answer sounded, the stranger thing was that it did not deter nor surprise her.

"Do you carry mine too?" Jade scoffed.

"I don't carry them. I witness them", the woman answered in the same soft even tone.

Jade turned around to look at her this time. She didn't know why, when their eyes met, a kind of familiarity she could not explain surfaced. Was it the color of the dress, because she loved white? Was it the expression of the face, somewhat motherly?

"What's the difference? And it doesn't make sense anyway. Your witness does not alleviate my pain."

Her eyes did not leave Jade's, and falling into her eyes Jade fell into a well of inseparable expressions: loving, sad, amused? A cocktail of feelings she dared not fathom.

"I can feel your pain."

Suddenly Jade felt her anger rise at the stranger's calm expression. *No, you don't! Pain is personal. It's a place nobody other than the owner has the key.*

"I may not feel your pain the way you experience it," the Lady-in-White continued like she could read minds, "but I understand love and happiness. And the happiness you call yours, is just an illusion because it comes and goes. If it truly is, it must be present all the time wherever you are."

Jade could not profess that love was happiness, but it sure was one of its facets, for she knew how happy she could be when he was around, and how hellish it was after he left.

With the hurt, the uncertainty of ever finding true love plagued her since she learned breakups were not accidental. The underlying mismatch came up to the surface, when the circumstances for truth to bare all were favorable. But didn't she do what everyone did? Take the opportunity at happiness whenever it offered itself, hoping the good times

14

would outweigh the bad, rather than wasting time waiting for a perfect match, a perfect love that might never materialize. Did not everyone take risks when they set sail for a new relationship?

She looked at her hands to avoid looking at her interlocutor, her mumbling barely audible.

"He said he loved me, and one day, that stopped without any plausible explanation. He was my happiness. And then he cheated on me. I hate him!" Tears started to run down, the vocal admission of hurt finally broke the dam of pride and self-preservation.

"Making somebody the God of your world is giving him a dreadful responsibility. He is not responsible for your happiness, nor for your sufferings. You are. You are responsible for your wanting and the consequences it brings. You are not his victim, he is not the perpetrator".

"Your wanting and expectations are your true enemies. Wanting something far too long it usurps and claims the right of a need. When the sightless need stays unanswered, it explodes causing the avalanche of emotions to bury you in pain".

Rational thinking could not erase the hurt, but the clinically cold, passionless analysis helped to impersonalize the deep emotion, made it factual, common, and banal. Bearable. Jade knew if she could only stop wishing things were the way they were, she would have found some peace.

She looked at the lady and asked: "Then how can I stop wanting?"

The answer came without missing a beat: "When you know wanting seldom brings home what you desire."

Wanting came to life in a dream Jade had last night. The rebellion against the impossibilities in life had converted into the parallel world of dreams.

They were together, strolling down the busy streets of Sai Gon, watching the colors of South-East Asia moving around them. Lingered at a bamboo hut cafeteria for a black café that could stop the heartbeat, savored a bowl of aromatic *pho* from the street vendors.

The voice called her back: "You know, you can't own a person."

Jade grimaced: "Not own."

The Lady-in-White smiled: "Wanting things to happen your way and your way only is the expression of selfish ownership. Entitlement. You cannot own a human and the core of his being, his emotions and feelings."

She had no answer to that. The aroma of her tea begged for tasting, and Jade slowly drank what she heard with it. She couldn't help but feel somewhat ridiculous, as the strange calmness of a patient accepting the much-feared diagnosis set in.

The smile never left her calm visage as the Lady-in-White brought the cup to her lips. The afternoon sun cast a golden light on her white long dress, created a shimmering aura around the table.

"Feeling lonely? Trying to run away from the solitude of your existence, you think?"

I don't know what to think. I miss him. And his presence, even if only as a witness to my solitude, is better than bearing it alone.

But Jade simply said: "Loneliness is a cancer that eats at people's lives. It is a void that love can help fill in."

"That can be done, but only by you. Love from someone else distracts from that inherent loneliness, but is not the solution. Why? Who else but you can fathom the depth of that solitude to find the perfect solution? To fill it with the love for yourself. You can try to look for an outside connection, but hoping that an outside presence will replace the emptiness inside is fruitless."

Jade whispered: "But there are times when the pain of loneliness is as real as this world, and I long for the love from somebody besides myself."

Sorrow filled the answer: "People's minds are narrowed by their perceptions, conditioned by the experiences they encountered, so finding a true connection is hazardous. You look at each other but sadly you don't see each other."

The encounter with an eagle on one solitary hike not long ago rolled back in Jade's mind. It was not rare to see these majestic wings on the trail, but she had never seen one in motion at such close range. She stopped dead when she spotted it above the shrubs, at a turn of the mountain dirt road. She admired in solemn stillness as the large bird floated in the air a few feet above her head. She could see the rugged line of demarcation where the white feathers of the neck smoothed over its mocha body, a precious moment that made her feel connected, chosen. Then it circled up in its unmistakable flight pattern to reach the sky. Her heart followed it, circle after circle, higher and higher, graceful yet powerful, until it became a dark spot in the vaporous sky, and shot as an arrow, straight to its destination, a place beyond her dreams. The ritual in the sky was a soaring solitude, an exalted call of freedom. Why was it, that with her, solitude became a yoke, solitude turned into loneliness?

The Lady-in-White spoke: "Solitude is not the problem. The fear of solitude is. If you accept solitude as part of the human condition, then your love will be liberated from an intimate need of escaping. That is the start of compassion.

"There is no love without compassion. Without compassion love is a barren terrain where the fire of anger, competition, egos, one-sided truth, right and wrong destroy the little life that is there. Love without compassion is possession that shies away from its true name."

Jade: "You mean true love?"

The Lady-in-White: "We can't say true love for love can't be untrue, but love and compassionate love".

Jade mused over the thought. She looked around the coffee shop now as empty as her feeling inside. The lady's voice soft as a caress of light:

"The loneliness you feel, or awareness of one's existence, is a gift viewed as a curse. You may run away from it, cover it with hope, with love, with what makes you happy for a short moment, and manage to mask it. But whenever one thinks of oneself as a separate entity, one imprisons oneself within the walls of loneliness.

"The truth is our breath reverberates within the whole universe. The fear of change engenders the hope for stability. Hope for stability is neither peace nor happiness.

"The ground we walk on is not a sturdy ground. How can we expect immobility in a moving world? If we take that clinging to stability off for a mere second, all false identifications will fall away, we will be one with truth. In that second, we are Perfection, Love, and Compassion.

"Love is a gift. To expect how a gift should be is ingratitude. Love is an expression of compassion reaching out from the shell of Ego, the Self and Selfishness to touch another manifestation of Life. It touches You. That moment...

"That moment, be it as brief as the touch of a butterfly or as long as the lifetime of a rock, is real, is truth. It is the trapdoor which time lets you peer into

Timelessness and shall be remembered as true, the ugliness of the world after that glimpse is but futile and irrelevant."

On those words, she waved for the waiter. After the Lady-in-White had gone, Jade lingered outside the shop, trying to live this moment when the heart found fewer obstacles to peace.

Like anything else in this world, what had a birth would have a death. So did love. Sometimes the life of a love did not extend to the length of our existence, sometimes it did. If the love he had for her died too soon against all promises, she should accept the death of their relationship as a Life course revelation. She made the choice, she bought the lottery ticket.

Her love was also a gift, but she had brandished it over the receiver like a sword and burdened him with her giving. She held it against him and created a prison of expectations that slowly took its life away. Love could not breathe in a cage. It was not always possible to revive a fire that had been extinguished, and false hope prevented her from accepting that the end had arrived and that she needed to turn the page.

Jade thought of the unnamed fear, hidden under a forcefully detached demeanor, of the first dates. The first time was always awkward, unwholesome, wonderful. Hope in its purest form, for the heart was open to the unknown. It thumped, accelerated, and missed a beat. She could keep that momentary truth in its pristine state in an untouched corner of her memory, and move on with the tide of events. She could let go.

Jade's errant mind had led her steps to the large fountain carved in travertine at an intersection. The ornate, imposing scene in the center commanded admiration and respect.

Lights illuminated the gigantic baroque statue from under the bubbling water. Impervious to human turmoil, the impassible Ocean in person looked beyond our fate into the infinite, indifferent to the messengers on both sides controlling the pull of the horses to his chariot: two opposing forces, yin and yang, strong and weak, day and night, sorrow and happiness, the dichotomy of everything.

It was believed that throwing a coin in this fountain would ensure a return to this city, the city of Love. *Why not?* Jade reached inside her purse, searched until she felt the cold touch of a coin. Then turned her back to the august Oceanus on his imposing chariot, she threw the coin over her left shoulder. The plop sound when the coin hit water made her smile.

Tracing her steps back to the train station, Jade contemplated the ruins again before leaving. The imposing shapes stood darker than night, but not so ambiguous, not so desperate anymore, tender relics of thousands of lives, who had loved and accepted the price of love, the price of living.

The City of Friendship

The train slowed down with the blaring whistle, another city on the long itinerary. Loud music invaded the train cars when it stopped and doors cracked open. Smiles and laughter added to the noise as long lost friends hugged each other catching up on old times. A few tears here and there but for Jade, anger and sadness. The perspective of this stop had kept her long awake the night before, and when finally her sleep came, it wavered to the lullaby of bitterness.

None of her sisters lived at a drop-by distance, so her friends straddled the undetermined line where friends stopped and family started. And Jade belonged to the quasi-extinct breed of romantically loyal people. Believing loyalty as the essence that bonded unrelated strangers to a life long closeness worsened the wound. Her friend should have stayed away from her husband. Her friend should have helped when she could instead of taking credit when Jade did the work. Her friend should have ...

Clumps of passengers formed and dispersed on the platform, some disappeared into the backseats of small cars, some in black cabs.

A scarlet double-decker bus approached and swerved to a stop at the curb where her group stood, the unmistakable tourist flock, with flashing and dangling cameras, a constant amazed air on their faces, high pitched voices too excited to stay in the normal graver tone. Jade was the last one to get on the bus behind a tall man in a dark gray raincoat, a little out of place in this weather, but to each his own, and everybody looked good in a trench. Today the sun was generous, bestowed on the earth a rare clear and warm day that could almost be happiness to some. No window seat left. No surprise.

The tour bus weaved through the narrow streets of the city, heading to the north side of the dark green river. The driver dropped them off at the gate of a castle known for its history of a lust-driven king who beheaded his queen.

Jade was slow to work up the curiosity for the horrific story of betrayal in an over crowded tourist must-see. Leaving the loud group marching towards the entrance, she went the opposite direction, to the riverbank bordered by coffee gardens. She walked by the tempting smell of coffee and inviting white chairs, but the company of a crowd was neither tempting nor inviting. The crowd was attractive only when one had a familiar face to forget it with.

Jade followed a narrow path along the river back to the street. She hailed a black cab, hoping for a place where the quiet and the new could cohabit.

"Good day, Madam. Beautiful day, isn't it? Where would you like to go?"

The old world, old era politeness of the old cabbie made Jade smile, the first of this long morning. *Madam likes to go where the locals go.*

Instead Jade said: "I'd like to visit your beautiful gardens. Which one do you recommend?"

And she marveled at the knowledge of the chatty driver about his city; he exulted a sense of belonging that made this city much more alive than any propaganda could.

"If Madam has time," … and he went on describing and detailing the gardens and historic castles attached to them… She settled for one not far away from the train station.

The large varieties of plants in numerous gardens in the park overwhelmed Jade's senses. Many flowers whose names she did not know opened in colors she did not think existed in nature. In one parterre, camellias in all the earth old nuances of pink, from almost white to deep sweet pink, to newer breeds of spotted hybrids, delighted the eyes. Camellia, the flower Jade had come to love, because of the sound of its name and the book '*La dame aux camelias.*' Huddled together, they looked fragile, like the book's character Marguerite.

The garden's complex layout contrasted with the unassuming symmetrical architecture of the palace in its center. It loomed behind the tall trees that bordered the pathways converging to its front courtyard. Purple crocuses in bloom formed a tender carpet at the feet of the vigorous trees. Fragrance came from everywhere, the ground, the trees, the air, and it smelled purple, the color of sadness.

The long walk pushed her anger aside, but sadness remained.

"Hypocrite!" she scolded, venting in solitude, a healthy and addictive habit she had developed through the years of living alone.

A familiar voice startled her: "You pay for your choice, or lack of choice."

Jade recognized this voice! She turned around and looked at a lady walking towards her. The Lady-in-White. To her own surprise, Jade sort of expected this kind of strangeness from this lady. Her heart didn't have any space left for surprise, only the joy of seeing a face who had already become familiar.

"In a way you said I made the choice to be betrayed?" Jade asked as a greeting.

The Lady-in-White smiled at Jade, the same indulgent smile one had for children. Tenderness without condescendence.

"You said she betrayed you but you keep the friendship going."

Jade said: "It's hard to break away from somebody who has been in my life for such a long time."

"Somebody who shouldn't be in your life in the first place. You don't choose your friends, you let circumstances chose for you."

Yes, there was no denying of that. Jade was not choosy when friends were involved. She would try to bond with any person she crossed paths with, out of need of human warmth. Sometimes the burgeoning friendship developed into something meaningful. Sometimes it became deformed, drained her optimism and trust in people. Friends were there for heartbreaks. She did not suspect they were heartbreaks themselves.

The wind played with the long dress of Jade's companion as they walked to a bench and sat down. Saucer magnolias in full bloom of pink perfumed the air around them. Wrought iron benches bordered the walk at intervals and softened the concrete way to the red palace.

Feelings were the brushwork of Van Gogh, colorful, impressionistic, blinding. But for beauty to integrate with reality, feelings needed to be defined, a drawing with the finite lines of an architect's plan.

Jade had found herself falling head over heels for people who she should not have, for some people simply had too many lovable traits, and the heart has never been known for being rational. But she had not built any relationship on the shards of someone else's happiness, especially of friends. She would not have allowed herself the breach of trust. It was not easy, it was hell, but not impossible. Why couldn't Claudia do the same? Lower moral standards?

Morals in essence were self-respect. Cheaters only had respect for their desire, and lies were the only instrument that could breathe reality into their want. Jade liked to live under the sun, and lies were nasty insects that only thrived in the damp darkness. As a friend, she should have forgiven that friend, or not?

The Lady-in-White's voice cut through her reflection: "Friends are people who at some point in your life cross your path and add warmth to your existence, add meaning to things that were insignificant. They are the moon when your lover is the sun, always there, even when you forget about them. They are the secret garden you relax in when the storms of life howl around you. They don't carry your burden but they can be the support that helps you carry yours. They are the whiff of wild flowers you catch on a hike. And you are the same for them.

"Along the way, something will change; along the way, some friends will drop out; along the way, impermanence will turn the ship of your life in a new direction, and friends depart. No blaming, for it stems from the unconscious expectation. When you say expectation, you're saying Me."

Jade asked, her voice softened: "Then what should I do with friends who fall out, who develop insane jealousy, who are wickedly competitive, who don't behave like friends anymore? I think some loyalty is expected in friendship."

"Friends who are not loyal are not true friends. They're friendly acquaintances that may need you for some ulterior motives, with every element of a business deal using friendship as currency. Bad friends are poison coated in sugar, chocolate, whatever bait that you're susceptible to."

"It's always too late when you find out." That friends could hurt friends. That friends could be dormant enemies.

It was so strange, on this quiet Sunday in a park greener than hope, talking about heartbreak by seemingly insignificant things. Anguish and bitterness have faded away, fallen somewhere at the outline of civilization, at that train station.

She asked: "What can I do?"

"What needs to be done to undo friendship?"

"No, but I don't know how to be friends and be detached enough to not to get hurt."

"What causes hurt is your expectation – unconscious expectation. As with love, friendship is a gift. A friend is a gift life has indulged you with. Things happen because a thought has materialized. Friends distance because knowing or unknowingly, a bitter grain has fermented in the shadow of trust. If the tenderness has died with friends who leave the friendship shore, you should thank them for the past, where the bond has created good memories, for the present that will not last, and for the future that will not hold any hurt from them.

The Lady-in-Whit paused, then continued: "Remember, friends are not the answer to your loneliness. They are the roads parallel to yours, but not the same one. Let there be space in your bond. Let the difference be the fresh air that blows life into that tie. And don't expect them to be the friend you are. Then a heart without resentment will free you from sufferings. And what about true friends? You forget them when you dwell on friends who are soon-to-be-exes. You spend time thinking of what was there instead of what is now."

Jade knew the Lady-in-White was right.

When she settled into her tiny house after her divorce, Mia was pregnant with her second child. That did not stop her from picking up new furniture at a discount store for Jade with her husband's truck. Two women and a *Miss Dolly Fourwheel* could accomplish a lot of moving. Then they patted themselves on the back: "Hey, we don't need men for muscles stuff!"

And Lan who, on weekends, showed up at her door at the crack of dawn in full gear: hat, garden gloves and long sleeve shirt, when she started the taming of weeds.

Millions of other small things that friends did for each other, easily forgotten in the stream of constant new needs. Jade kept thinking about no-good friends, was it the survival instinct twisted by a form of sadistic behavior that she displayed? Going back to problems believing she could fix the past. Went back to the pain, physical or emotional, like an addict. Kept touching the sore tooth, reliving the painful experience, thinking of what hurt instead of what soothed. If she decided to put herself in the victim chair, she should be able to afford the discomfort.

Friends were there for many reasons, but most of all, for moral support to soothe the aching need of acceptance. To find a friend is to find a limpid heart for the mind to look at the reflection of itself.

"Don't close your heart and reserve your affection for the sole people you call friends. Extend it to people who are not your friends by definition, but your paths have crossed and their act leaves an imprint in your life. Their presence and attitude towards the world makes them true friends of the world, and you. They're friends without the possessive adjectives you like to stick on relationships.

The Lady-in-White paused, looked at the dusty roses that smiled at her from a parterre and continued:

"Form a friendship with the Earth, the Air, the Sun, the ground you walk on. Anything you touch, forms a friendship with Life.

"Make friends with the world you live in. Don't hate it or the people in it. If you hate people, you also hate yourself, because the world is a reflection of

34

yourself. Look for ugliness and you'll find *ugly*. Look for friendliness and you'll find *friends*. You looked for colors and beauty, you found this park. You looked for answers, you found me."

Jade brushed a leaf off her shoulder as her eyes followed the dance of a swallowtail flirting with the wide magnolias. It made her think of strangers whose acts had kept her oscillating belief in humanity strong.

She remembered the genuine smile of strangers on the street that raised a decimal on the barometer in a chilly day. People who paid attention to infinitely small details of life and made it worth each breath. The butterflies of the world, flying flowers in search of the too busy and the too tired who did not stop for beauty anymore. If she wanted, she could see them everywhere.

People who have left their footprints in the world throughout time, the immense change following the breakthrough they made, the better condition they left for mankind, the insignificant impact of her own on other people's life, but glad to be a witness.

People who gave their fortune of time and money to better others' lives. People who believed higher education should be free and worked on their belief. Beautiful people spoke in many ways. She could inhabit her world with unfriendly people or gravitate towards the light, her choice, her doing.

Suddenly the park felt quieter, the scattered tourists had long gone for lunch at the food court on the other side of the park. Jade heard her heart beat discreetly like excusing itself for making noise in the meditative silence. Her heart. It never stopped beating since the day she was formed, and it would continue to beat until the day it would be too tired to go on. Each beat was a sound of loyalty, in a body that she more often then not took for granted. It was a forgotten friend, in a friendship that internalized the warmth instead of spending it, and like flame fed on flame, it nourished itself. It lived on trust.

"You know who is there for you but never gets the attention and thanks much deserved?" The Lady-in-White asked in her soft but clear voice.

Jade hurried: "Mia?"

The Lady-in-White looked at Jade, slightly shook her head.

"Lan?"

"Yourself, Jade."

Jade's head jerked away, for her words jolted dark memories, and the past gradually drifted back.

The time when darkness was loving and comforting, when light and laughter hurt. The arms of the dark sheltered her crying, her planning sanguinary revenge, her daydream of suicide. Until the day she finally decided happiness was a choice like any trivial choice. She made the choice of leaving the divorce embitterment and male hating with the dark.

Remembering the time when her mother passed away. The news hit her as only a runaway train could. The home she could always go back to for love and peace was destroyed. The first time Jade knew how orphans felt. Spring died with her mother's death.

Solitary hikes kept getting longer and lonelier. Then came that day. The same sun rose on the same horizon at the same cardinal point, but she woke up to the mortality of all the ones she loved and realized that memories were the family inheritance that would live on. And her mother was alive in her good genes, in the smiles of her sisters, in the way her brother nodded. She was certain her happiness would be her mother's happiness, and the forced smile became more and more natural with time.

She was there for Her. In the past, in the present and no doubt would be in the future. She was never alone. The most loyal friend she could hope for had never left her side, had never deserted her, had never let her down. A feeling of gratitude overwhelmed her.

Jade looked at the Lady-in-White, her eyes swelled with unshed tears: "Thank you."

"No, thank You."

A leaf fell on the bench where they sat. The wind played with it for a while then rolled it away. The day has gone to sleep behind the ragged horizon of the city, and night was tiptoeing in to claim its place. Hope played hide-and-seek somewhere behind the corners of darkness. In a minute, she would be back on that train, but her mind would still be here, on this bench. Her thoughts fell into the crack of time, where past, present, and future, were a circle with no end or beginning.

The City of Aging
on the Outskirts of Beauty and Youth

Jade woke up frazzled, her thirty years on Earth weighed like the Earth itself. It had been a normal night and a normal morning like any other day, but distress had somehow crept in to disturb her sleep. She had breakfast in the dining car, chewed on a pre-made meal without remembering its taste, avoiding eye contact with other passengers. The train was approaching Aging City.

They would stay here for a few days, then they would continue on their long way to the last city on the trip's schedule, the last stop, the ultimate destination.

Off the train, Jade dragged the suitcases along the uneven stone path to the hotel on the main street, in the heart of the chic quarter.

The impassible greeter who stood guard in front of the hotel opened the door with a slick movement. The big hotel facade presented a mix of neo-renaissance and baroque style that could read grandiose to some, and ostentatious to others. To her, its pretention was odious. A round rug with intricate pattern, Persian perhaps, decorated the center of the large golden lobby designed to make travelers feel intimidated and lost. The long golden oak check-in counter on the left added weight to the imposing décor. The vault opposite the entrance opened to the view of the ocean. The sound of the waves rushed in, through the blood of eager travelers.

Waiting for her turn, Jade watched the line and the plump-lipped clerk. Her lips were too plump even for a twenty something. Long fake lashes gave the eyes a certain mysterious gaze, and her attitude, that of arrogance derived from good looks, paired with reluctant politesse required by the job, resulted in a disfigured condescendence. Jade tried not to show interest in the couple in front of her. The man, if he were a woman, or if he could carry, would have been well in his fourth month of pregnancy. He kept the line halted and annoyed faces grown in number by asking questions that did not need to be asked, waiting for the answers that did not need to be spelled out. His chubby companion's exasperation threatened to turn into a verbal fit of anger; she opened her mouth, closed it, rolled her eyes, opened her mouth again, shrugged and closed it again. Jade told herself: *Somebody will not be enjoying the sea today.* She averted her eyes as she got to the counter, the last obstacle before the well-deserved rest.

Leaving the suitcase with the valet, she took the stairs up. The thick oak planks resonated under her heels, echoing her every thought.

Aging was not fun at all. Anybody who said aging posed no problem to them did not know how deep the abyss was before jumping to conclusions, or they were lying. *Browning, you're wrong.*

How much money people are willing to spend trying to stop this natural course of life? Open the suitcase of any traveler. One is sure to find some products that help with looks. Chemically and surgically enhanced people perpetrate the madness. The madness for youth. Even youth itself subscribes to it. The beautiful becomes perfect. The older in comparison becomes sin-ugly.

41

Now 'the older' was met in front of her room by the valet and her suitcases. Jade gave him a generous thank you note and settled into her temporary home.

As Jade washed her face, she examined the lines under her eyes, in the well-lit, cold and tactless mirror of the bathroom.

She did not care if wrinkles gave character, she would rather not have them, because the price for that character was invisibility. Especially if the cloak of invisibility fell upon her in an unexpected moment at a party, where she was happy and chatty, and turned to her partner to see his antenna light up to a thousand watts at the sight of a much younger woman. His indifference to her presence invalidated her existence.

Unable to lie in bed with thoughts racing in her mind, Jade put on her bikini and went down to the swimming pool. The water had a calming effect that she would welcome instantly.

The mosaic laid swimming pool was artsy enough to exude a unique charm and friendly feel. Balustrade and ficus trees in large terracotta planters separated it from an adjacent covered terrace.

Lounge chairs and parasols populated a wide platform on the opposite side.

No one here but Jade and a young couple. She settled at one of the round tables on the terrace to drink the chamomile tea she brought down with her. She stared at the swimmers breaking the calm surface of the blue water with their strokes. The young woman and her companion reached the shallow water, and her red bikini emerged. From the back Jade could see a very small waist that had not known maternity and high placed buns that had not known gravity. Long legs that the little Mermaid would have deemed worth the stabbing pain propelled the evenly tanned body onto the mosaic edge of the pool. The lithe creature now standing in all its young glorious perfection, facing her beau, made him laugh with what Jade guessed was a witty remark.

Why now? Jade grasped the warm cup and drank her bitterness.

"Are you hungry yet?"

This voice... Jade turned to its direction and saw the Lady-in-White making the last steps to her table. Jade was too happy to see her, the feeling of cool shade much needed in this moment of burning pain. She eagerly nodded and put on her wrap.

They followed the graveled path alongside the hotel to the restaurant in back. The eternal sound of the waves grew louder as they approached, playing a soothing note on her somber mood.

They sat down just outside of the restaurant at a small wooden table, its fat round center leg half buried in the white sand. It did not take long for the waitress to come, the beach was still deserted, the crowd was still in the process of making home in the hotel.

Jade couldn't help but resume her dark thought: "Aging is terrible."

"Yes?"

"One becomes invisible with age. That makes one feel unwanted, unloved."

"By who?"

"By everybody...well, by the other sex."

Now that Pandora's box was open, the odor of the exposed truth stained every word.

"By my partner. Not exactly that, but..."

The waitress with an undulant walk came back with their orders, saved her the embarrassment of a confession. The grilled pink salmon was displayed in a square white plate, sprinkled with white speckles of garlic, a couple of green asparagus curved on the side to complete the tableau. On her companion's plate, the eggplant still had a purple color that the grill had not turned into café au lait, and on the opposite side, peppered glass noodles. The presentation was zen-ly beautiful, like everything else in the Lady-in-White's presence. It was as if she had the power to erase the world of any impurity.

She said: "You said old age is the curse of relationships?"

Jade admitted: "I only seriously think about this whole age thing since I saw my partner's interest in younger women. Of course he lied about it. He was interested in the dynamics of human interactions, he said, even when the young and attractive woman was alone!"

The lady rolled the glass noodles on her fork then asked: "Do you like the food?"

"What…huh …yes!" Surprised, Jade answered automatically.

They ate in silence. Forced to be in the moment, food did taste as it was: deliciously savory.

45

The fruit of unconditional love from the Earth, with a touch of human love.

"Human beings are naturally attracted to Beauty." The Lady-in-White conceded.

"Beauty in any form." Jade added.

"You are conditioned by your Self to perceive Beauty the way you do. Most people identify Beauty with Youth. Your ego suffers the attention you don't get, not because of beauty or age itself."

Jade tried to digest what she has just heard. It rang too close.

"You could be right."

The Lady-in-White looked at Jade. She had the appearance of a defeated soldier who has accepted his destiny.

"It's not youth you desire. Imagine this, that society is structured differently, women are valued solely by the fruits of their work, and that gives them let's say fame; which is intelligence and talent culminated into recognition, or material success; which is experience matured into tangible abundance, or by wisdom; digested thoughts culminated into a way of living with poise and serenity, then the desirability would not be youth. On the contrary, it would be the maturity of age, that dimension of time, which engendered all that success".

"Chimerical! That will never happen! It's not the reality of this society, or this world".

"You make this society's reality yours. You carry the yolk this society has enslaved you with, thinking you are free. But deep layers of fear tie you up. Drowning in the rest of the world's regulations on your behavior, bound by your own abiding to those conditions. You have to have a partner because you fear being seen as unwanted. You have to do something special because you fear that your whole existence has no real meaning".

"That is a scary thought, a life with no real purpose".

Jade looked away at the beach goers who started to populate the stretch of white sand along the restaurant. She recognized a family on her train, which reminded her of the couple in the hotel lobby, wondered if they would be here soon, if they had sailed through the rocky shore of their relationship. From the corner of her eyes, she saw her companion stand up and walk to the hut that housed the bar and the cashier's counter. Her svelte form in the all white dress seemed to float on the sea of sand, her steps light as feathers. Jade sighed. It would take her light years of evolvement to be where her companion was now. For the present time, she yearned for the elusive attention that youth and beauty offered.

Jade made a few steps in her direction as she saw the Lady-in-White headed out.

The lady said: "Go for a walk?" Jade nodded and followed her.

She asked: "Where were we?"

Jade said: "I think if I were younger, I would be more desirable. I could avoid the heartache."

"Each individual has his or her own perception of desirability. Most people will find youth desirable. Classical beauty desirable. People from a different mold find integrity, charisma of character desirable. The eyes of the beholder, depends on the degree of the mental development and the spiritual evolvement of the person, and will stay in the three dimensional world or transcend beyond the touch, see, smell and taste."

There was something solid in her arguments. Jade did find compassion, kindness very attractive, very sexy. It touched her deeper and truer than the feeling for a beautiful body.

Leaving the restaurant behind, they strolled along the beach. Jade dug her feet in the wet sand, feeling the comforting touch.

Her companion broke the silence: "Can you say this with conviction: I am older age-wise, therefore I am wiser? I had helped others and have more to offer, I don't wait to live for I am living now. I don't envy younger people because I have been there and know the price of not knowing. Can you?"

It took Jade a few steps before the thought sunk in. That, *that* was too bold of a statement. Reading her thoughts, the Lady-in-White continued:

"Will you face your fears now? Fear cripples you. It dictates your behavior. It stalks your every thought. It bolts you down where you want to soar. It silences your voice when the lyric of your heart is ready on your lips. It's the unrequited love you need to let go of for peace of mind to be found."

Jade knew that her fear was so well masked that even she was duped. The fear of not being good enough to deserve love. But it was the sort of secret she'd rather it not be discovered or named.

"It's the dirty laundry that I don't want to wash under the sun", Jade admitted.

The Lady-in-White smiled, "Only You think that it's a secret."

Jade couldn't help but laugh. At that moment, suddenly all the dirty laundries of the world were unrolled in front of her. Fear and pain in every face she has met, close ones and strangers, friends and not-quite-so, rich and poor, old and young, the accused and the accuser, the changing face of Fear. A sense of oneness overcame her. A tender love enveloped the moving sea of faces. We were equal in pain. We were not enemies. Our common enemy was Fear.

"Fear is universal. Another disease that plagues humanity," Jade said.

"Every disease carries a cure in itself. Think of bacteria and vaccination. Two sides of the same coin. Equally important and equally non-existent. The name is given to differentiate the elements in that state of dichotomy. To what extent, what length, what height are you willing to explore these opposites to find the answer?"

Jade: "Exploring fear is a fearful task!"

The lady: "Exploring fear negates fear."

They headed back to the hotel, small steps on the sand, seawater caressing their feet. The forever chant of the ocean impregnated Jade's thoughts, slowly washed away layers and layers of worries. *I could go to sleep right now.*

"I'll see you tomorrow. Goodnight."

Jade thought she heard the farewell before sliding into the arms of a complete silence.

* * *

Lying in bed, she watched the morning crawl in with short, silent steps of light. She was sad and ashamed of herself. Fear of being hurt had her torturing herself and the one who loved her. Fear of abandonment had created insurmountable obstacles between her heart and true love. How did she operate? *As long as my heart is intact, I am safe.* Knowing that she could have been unfair resulted in a heavy doubt about her own worth. In every breakup, she had contributed her part. She finally got up.

The face that looked back from the bathroom mirror was not a well rested one, but the sparkle in her eyes made up for the lack of freshness. Jade changed into her favorite swimming suit, slipped the cover on and went to the beach.

She could see the Lady-in-White standing on the beach, watching the calm water. An apparition in white against the shimmering blue of the sky and the sea. She turned to look at Jade then led the way.

It was a wonderful feeling, that of following a stranger who became so close so fast, following an unknown person with the anticipation that all her problems would soon be solved, her questions would be answered, where she would find peace, even if it was for a short and transient moment. Happiness is not a rock with absolute dimensions to make it solid for a foundation, but the fleeting beauty of a butterfly's wings. She felt like she was following a cloud.

They walked in the busy morning of waking restaurants, passed the streets of burgeoning noise, to the quieter area, to the hills.

Jade could not hold any longer, she turned to her companion and eagerly shared: "I think I came to terms with aging."

"You did", the question had no question mark in the tone.

"Yes. Aging is not that scary anymore. I can fight it my own way and find happiness within it."

"Then how do you fight old age?"

"I don't fight anymore. I accept it."

"Do you see the beauty in it?"

"Not beauty, but its benefit for peace of mind. Experiences gathered with age are valuable knowledge for survival, for a happier life."

"Very well spoken. Will you have plastic surgery one day?"

Jade glanced at her, not answering. They were going up a hill covered in green bushes. The winding red dirt trail on this steep slope disappeared into the lush green tapestry at the top. And above them, the immense blue palace. Her steps were slow and precise.

"No. I don't see the reason". Jade added with a smile: "I did think about it before."

"You accept old age like you accept a defeat. But it's not a defeat and aging has its own beauty."

Jade breathed through her mouth. It was not always easy to be read like an open book, one needed some mystery, a certain wall to cover one's nakedness.

"You were not born with clothes."

"It's instinctive to try to protect oneself."

"Yes, but is there a place to hide?" The Lady-in-White continued: "Don't feel ashamed of aging. That feeling of shame is anything but instinct. Don't look at your acceptance that aging is a seemingly inevitable natural process the way you look at fate. That is the way of a defeated and small mind, not the way of a warrior who has won the battle and is setting out for the sky. You don't see beauty in its true form, that's why you don't see the beauty of age.

"Beauty can manifest in any form, in that yellow flower". She pointed at the bright, brave touch of sun on the side of the road nodding at them in the light breeze.

"Beauty can manifest in a smile or a tear. Beauty can be the color black or the color white. Beauty doesn't need to step on the pedestal called ugliness to be crowned Beauty. It is true so it doesn't have to settle in any fixed form. If dimensions limit beauty then it's a limited beauty. If beauty is limited by time then that beauty is only a fraction of timeless beauty. If beauty is youth then that beauty is borrowed.

"Age, sickness, death… you should examine them as misfortune and also as opportunity. Only then will you be able to find balance and joy."

The sun was high above them, but the cool breeze blew the heat away, left a perfect day behind its trail.

"What if the numbers of our age scare us?"

"If the numbers stare at you, look straight back at them and ask: "So what?" Does your laughter have age? Do your tears? Does your compassion? Does your anger? Your true Self is ageless."

Jade kept silent, but felt relieved.

The Lady-in-White left Jade to the hot sand and the warm sea heated by the ripe sun. As she swam out to the horizon, the waves formed on the wake of each stroke dispersed her concentration on old age and brought back enjoyment. She floated on the languid water, looking at the white cloud floating on the ethereal ocean. Which world was real?

Jade went back to the hotel at sunset. The bar in the lounge greeted her with the smile of a dark haired bartender.

"Vodka dirty martini. Up with Blue cheese olives. Please." She needed a rush in her body to match the rush in her mood.

The glass was separately chilled, the cheese was fresh, the dirty looked just right. Perfect night.

The immaculate towels stacked on the shelves above the shower emanated an aura of cleanliness as they reflected in the bathroom mirror.

Lying in the bathtub, Jade listened to the running water slowly filling up, covering her body inch by inch with its warm embrace. A very different sound from the lament of the sea. A brief relief from the natural course, birth old age sickness and death, this 'man made' sound suddenly became familiar, reassuring, and peace was now.

Beauty and Youth

5 The authentic Mexican food restaurant packed its waiting area and dining halls with thick smells and talking crowds. The three friends, chatting, laughing, waited for their table in the dark red brick portico. Isabella and Jessica picked Jade up for lunch to introduce her to this hot spot, a restaurant with the kind of dishes that drove people out of their food comfort zone straight into the cosmopolitan ethnic food world.

The host talked to Isabella. She was tall, with elegant long legs to have a graceful walk, but not so tall as to look most guys eye-to-eye. Earth round saline breasts blown to the proportion of her hopes.

Thick, luscious wavy hair framed the face of a modern Titian's Flora, with taut skin worked by cosmetics to the point that no trace of epidermis was visible. Her mane fell with abandonment on her cream white shoulders, caressing her elongated neck on the downward passage. She moved with natural grace in a bandage dress, the strategic cut of the dress enhanced her magnetic curves, and an off-white Gucci tote dangled from a leisure hand with well-manicured fingers. Jade cringed in her nearly flat-chest body, tried to be comfortable on the sideway of the searing attention shot at her friend as they weaved their way behind the host through a sea of full tables, shapely legs, and flashes of content faces.

As luck decided to be generous whenever Isabella was around, they got a table by the window looking out over an exotic garden. The flower baskets hung at different heights filled the space with fresh faces of geraniums, columbines, and Venus orchids. It was a dance of colors and fragrances, for the shutters were opened to let the perfume swirl in.

A waiter came over with a nonchalant sunny morning smile, the same way he moved, if one could compare facial expression to gait. Isabella handled the orders and the flirting as always.

Then the conversation jumped from boyfriends, to husbands, to beauty and ended up on plastic surgery.

Isabella pondered: "I think everything has a price, and beauty can be bought. I bought mine." She boasted. "I had many surgeries and will have more. It's vanity to some people, but to me, it's a personal fight against that which robs me of my true self. I can't identify myself with wrinkles and sagging. Remember how I looked when I was in my twenties?"

"Yes, I do!" Jade drawled.

"Beautiful women don't have to work. That's what men are for." She snickered.

Jessica and Jade looked at each other, disturbed. They had seldom heard this fact declared with such candor. It took a certain kind of person to capitalize on their looks and admit it. Beautiful Isabella's honesty was disarming, alarming at times. But she was not a backstabber, and that quality was enough for friendship to last.

Her comment reminded Jade that she was alone, and for singles, dating was an ungrateful job. Whoever had played on the dating ground had known that lies were acceptable currency, and not everyone would wade through the troubled waters of relationship to find a genuine gem. Some people were even addicted to lies. Because lies were better than the truth. Man made beauty looked better than the natural kind because the surgical technology was space-aged advanced and the objective crystal clear. Nature threw carbon around with insouciance, catching that natural beauty was pure dumb luck. To be best armed for the game, one better lend nature a helping hand. Jessica pulled Jade out of her reverie:

"Acceptance will bring peace and contentment. If you are at peace with yourself, then it doesn't matter how you look. Beauty canon rests on pinwheels. Four, five hundred years ago in many European and Asian countries women with small breast were deemed beautiful. Then and now in most Asian countries fair skin is beauty while westerners see tan skin attractive. Most South Americans love women with a healthy derriere and so on. There may be a universal image of a physically perfect woman, but I doubt that everybody would agree on that. Ever heard of leg men or breast men?"

"Or butt men?" Jade added with a smile.

Isabella said, "I personally prefer horsemen."

Jade and Jessica looked at her, questions in the eyes. She shrugged: "It sounds better than stallion men."

Their laughter might have been too loud, even for this crowded place, for several glances from other tables shot at them.

Jessica continued: "My point is, you cannot always win in this fight. At some point you have to realize you must make peace with your look, or you'll still be fighting old age on your deathbed."

"That may be true, but to be desired feeds the ego. No, not ego, self-esteem." Isabella waved her hand and the thought of old age away, to the land of blissful ignorance.

Jessica put her glass down and casually said: "I'm happy with how I look, I'm happy with what I have."

Jade looked at her, reproach in the voice: "Jess, you are beautiful, and you are wealthy."

Jessica insisted: "I can always want more and make myself unhappy."

"Very true", Jade admitted.

They looked at each other and smiled. They didn't have answers to all of their questions, but they were having a good time, wishing in their hearts and in their smiles that their friends would have found happiness wherever it was. The path to happiness was a personal quest; the sole beneficiary would be the solitary pilgrim.

They had different lifestyles. Isabella simply did not work. There was always some lucky man too happy to take care of her needs. And she has always been very proud of what her beauty could bring: affection and 'things'. Jessica quit college and the side modeling gig during marriage then after her divorce, her ex-husband owned a clothing company so the alimony was substantial.

Jade was the workingwoman of the pack. The divorce did not end in her favor, because her ex husband could afford a lawyer and she couldn't. Since alimony and inheritance were non-existent and she disliked the idea of milking a relationship for commodities, she worked for everything she had, so she had to work. At times that made her feel underprivileged, but most of the time she felt free and proud. She was the boss of her financial destiny.

Except that at this moment, it tipped on the side of underprivileged.

After lunch Isabella dropped Jade off at the hotel. The heavy meal made Jade sleepy, the door of her room never looked more attractive and homey. She needed a siesta. And she desperately needed to talk to the mysterious Lady-in-White, because she was lost again. Jade hoped she would come to her rescue. The last thought hurried in as her eyes closed.

* * *

The late afternoon sun found Jade sitting on the sand, looking hard at the blue horizon as if waves would bring her some answers with the bobbling sea kelp approaching the white sand.

A hello made her head turn, the Lady-in-White was walking towards her. Jade stood up to greet her and they started their routine along the deserted beach. It was too late for beach lovers and too early for sunset watchers.

The Lady-in-White asked Jade in that soft and gentle voice that she never found to be condescending or overbearing:

"You seem pensive."

"I'm lost again. Do I envy those friends? Why do I envy them?"

"Do you think you have an identity crisis?"

"I don't understand."

"If you know who you are and how you want to live your life then you don't question it each time some alternative ways come into the picture."

"You're saying I envy those friends because I want their life?"

"Because you don't know what you want. Your friend's way of going through life is superficial, therefore no deep cut, somewhat painless; that seemingly painless life is envied, a life brought by purchased beauty. Bought and paid-for beauty mimics youth; youth itself is momentary. The reflection of a fleeting image, how lasting can that be? Pain shadows the relationship like a borrowed lover who slips away at every second."

"I envy them yet they're not really happy!" Jade had to admit to herself that the exclamation sounded almost joyful, like a cry of revenge. Then felt as deflated about herself as a poked balloon. Envy was ugly.

"Wanting prevents happiness", the Lady-in-White said softly.

Yes, I should not do that either. Looks or money. Wanting never knows the boundaries of Enough.

"Talk to me about the discrepancy of age in couples, please. Almost everybody goes for the young. Older women will be lonely because men her age are trading old partners for the newer models," Jade said.

"And vice versa. The insatiable thirst of the new-therefore-exciting exists as a condition of living. The thrill of the new makes living bearable, it bridges over existing dissatisfaction. It distracts from the true conditions of human beings. It's the denial of old age. People relive their youth in the possession of youth."

"Is that why women have plastic surgeries and men have partners their daughters' age?"

"Beauty is relative, so is youth. You always go back to relationships. Does that mean you put your worth in the successful outcome of a relationship?"

"Because if I was younger and more beautiful, I'd have a better chance at keeping love, a better chance in a relationship?"

"If a relationship means that much to you, every relationship is a risk. Why? Because their outcome controls your happiness, the prize you work hard to get. You think of yourself as an independent woman but you enslave yourself to the capricious Adonis."

Jade was silent.

Aging was not the simple fact of getting old. The decrease of physical beauty broke the dam that held the identity components together, and the flow of entangled underlying uncertainty surfaced. The *self* started to question *self*.

The beautiful-twenty-year-old-Jade suddenly became a stranger, a vague remembrance of some other life; Jade did not feel any connection with that individual. If she really was her, then this life was a dream! The identity she took now, this Me who was not existing at that time, would not be in the future, what really existed, were fractions of consciousness devoid of identity. She was not an unchanged entity.

Light in the sky started to dim, the promise of night was here, but dying sunrays were still flirting with the shapes of tall buildings.

Jade had to accept the fact that the body aged. She did not look like Jade-in-her-twenties. But she would not trade who she was at this time for that youth. Jade looked at that young girl whom she was, with the sort of tenderness and compassion people felt for somebody who was heading towards an abyss with insouciance. She did not know her youth was on loan.

So was the fate of every younger person she met. They would suffer from aging if not prepared. If they were lucky, they would meet a Lady-in-White of their own and understand the reality of youth and its flip side, old age. If they were not so lucky, they would only work on controlling the damage when the dam of age broke, hard work which was never done. Taking on gravity is a futile task.

The Lady-in-White said "True beauty is light. It's the inherent beauty that lightens everything around it, that can extract beauty from anyone it touches. That light cannot be extinguished by age."

Jade looked at the Lady-in-White and suddenly realized why she could not place her age nor why she thought of her as the most beautiful person she has met. Her mind shone through and defied matter.

The mind did not age, but matured with time. That mind was the light that animated the body.

Saying goodbye to the snakeskin of numbers, Jade sensed she has touched a being of light that has always been underneath but she was not aware of until now. If she could be one with that being, then the flow of truth would go on beyond death, another trick of the realm of forms.

It was getting dark, and the night was a tad chilly. They said goodbye and parted. Jade watched the Lady-in-White walk away, her silhouette seemed to be the last hope of the day, the last light that moved into darkness. Suddenly, she turned around and called softly with a smile:

"If you still think about plastic surgery, just know that surgically-enhanced beauty lacks the radiance of truth and the charisma of authenticity."

On that, she waved and faded into the night.

No. It's a fight for happiness. If I'm happy, I don't need a quick fix.

* * *

Morning had not set in yet, when Jade received a call from the lobby. Pierre and Bertha were here for the last breakfast in Aging town. It was not without nostalgia that she left this place and these friends.

Jade could see their smiling faces from the lobby as she walked by the balustrade of the first floor. Jade lingered at the top of the stairs while her heart already rushed down to meet Pierre.

They walked down the alley lined with small houses trying to wake up, a few windows reluctantly opened to the silent knock of the morning light. The coffee shop to which they were heading, was partially hidden under the climbing clematis. The vine danced all over its supporting wall, graciously invited the day through the open front door.

They chose a table on the veranda looking out at the blue water line. Bertha was a big boned dark clothed woman, with spiked hair the color of extinct red ashes. Her best feature was her personality and a face that carried her soul in her smile. At five feet five inches, when her weight swung between one hundred fifty and one hundred sixty pounds, she bailed out of the thinness cult, and dedicated to find happiness in self-acceptance. Jade admired her for the courage of going against the stream, at the same time questioned her friend's dedication to a goal. Jade was a ferocious achiever.

Jade and Pierre had dated for a while when she was in college. Jade brought the glass to her lips and discreetly looked at him. He hunched a little over his coffee cup, the table was too low for his frame. Pectoral muscles pushed up the tight brown t-shirt.

Brown hair cropped short to hide the curls but just a vain attempt. The broad, direct smile that did not know it rested on sensual lips. He had not changed since she last saw him.

"You don't look any different, you will age well, Pierre."

The tenderness in Pierre's eyes had not changed either: "You too. You're still the same. Aging? What? Why so depressing, Jade?"

"We should think about age at some point. But aging does not scare me anymore".

Pierre asked: "What is Aging to you?"

The ceramic cup of chamomile tea in her hands felt warm and comforting.

"The self that knows age is not the true self."

Both Pierre and Bertha raised their eyebrows. Bertha took a sip of coffee, put the cup down, then asked: "What is the true self?"

Jade: "The ageless self."

Pierre asked, "And what is That?"

"My joy doesn't have age, neither does my sadness. Come on, my orgasms don't have age!"

The three let out throaty laughs. Pierre shifted his position, leaned closer and said:

"I'm glad for you if aging does not bother you anymore."

"Yep. So no plastic surgery for me", Jade smiled.

"You don't need it."

"Nobody can afford to say that. But as far as plastic surgery goes, I'll only sign up for the one that I can perform."

"I'm not following."

"Plastic surgery as in cut up my credit cards."

Pierre smiled and shook his head, his eyes on Jade's face became more tender.

Bertha tapped on Jade's shoulder as she enunciated her words: "That means more money into the travelling fund. You need to come here more often to see us, Jade. Are you retiring from us?"

Jade yelled: "Silly!"

Pierre said: "I think plastic surgery is acceptable as long as it doesn't alter the physical appearance, if it enhances instead of changing."

"Of course you're pro, you're a man!" Both women chorused.

Pierre's face changed, a frown tried to pass as a smile, and fell short in between.

"At least I'm honest!"

"Yes, more honest than my ex-husband."

Jade frowned at the thought of her ex-husband. And frowned at her feelings for Pierre that did not automatically stop because she was in a relationship with another man. It did not manifest because of decency. And time with distance had helped to give decency the strength that it needed to stand up to emotions. The aroma of the tea brought her back: "He always said I don't like fake boobs, but then he remarked: 'When they're well done, they're spectacular!' But please remember, he's the ex now. Ex! Ax the ex."

"He didn't lie, what he meant was he did not like not-well-done fake ones." Bertha giggled.

"Don't penalize me for loving women. You like good looks too, don't lie."

Pierre still thought of a strategy to fend off Jade's imaginary attack. He developed his defense: "It's like food. I don't need to know how the dish is made to appreciate it. It's the same with plastic surgery. If the process does not change but enhances, then that beauty is not unlike natural.

"Yes. I do like hunks. But it doesn't mean that I will leave who I am with for a better-looking perspective." Bertha, like always dotted her *I*s and crossed her *T*s.

"Me neither." Pierre said. And looked at Jade in the eyes: "What do you like, Jade?"

"I don't like to be in a relationship where looks have to be kept up all the time to keep the other half's focus. It's like an everlasting battle."

"Men's surgeries are becoming popular too, and the trend is going strong." Bertha chimed in.

"Yuck!" Jade could not help to be judgmental.

"Yuck? You don't want a self-created Apollo? Not every guy is as handsome as I am." Pierre put in, as nonchalant as always.

Jade looked at the four inquisitive eyes, then looked down at her drink: "I want a man who was not popped out of some artificial womb with a newborn face. I want somebody whom each wrinkle on his face screams he's been struck by life, struck back, and is still standing. A man who has lived, has witnessed this life in its most beautiful and ugliest displays and yet free styles forward; a heart big enough to let the world with all its differences be, yet has enough integrity to abide to his own codes, and sculpts his existence into meaning. A man who knows words like love, affection ... in the end are amorphous, hollow, and molded his feelings into behavior towards his woman."

Bertha exclaimed: "Wow! When you find him, let me know, so that we can fight over the perfect specimen."

Pierre smiled as he volunteered: "He's right here, ladies! Right here."

The morning slipped fast away in laughter and affection on the North Shore, where they tried to catch a wave and an even tan.

Jade looked at Pierre dark and tall in the sun against the strong waves. Why was he still single? And why did she still feel awkward and shy around him? Who would he grow old with? Not with her, since she broke his heart once, and she doubted that he would give heartache another chance, but she was grateful that they stayed friends.

Growing old with somebody had to be a soulful fantastic experience. Trust, love, affection, integrity held hands to take the trembling couple into the age of serenity.

Jade remembered lovely old couples randomly seen in parks, in museums, that she hurried to forget because for a young and becoming woman, they were of no special interest, just a reminder that old age would creep up on her. Now, she only hoped that in her older years she could have that kind of a bond.

She had trapped her mind in the dependence of transient youth, shielded herself from the truth of age.

Dependence on youth and fleshy beauty attracted the same type of dependence into the relationship, and with that she expected true love. A deep love that even she did not have for herself, no wonder the past relationship was a failure. Relying on temporary assets and hoping for long term effect would never give Jade the kind of peace and poetry of walking the natural course with somebody once all the petals of youth has fallen.

She thought of the stratagem she and many others had been using.

The hook: looks. The content: intelligence, financial stability. She thought those were solid qualities for a rock stable commitment. Not integrity, compassion, patience, fairness, the necessary qualities that would have cemented two egos together. Jade might have some of those qualities, but did not think they were the most attractive attributes. After the hook has waned, and the contents unveiled they were not reliable, what left was the bare being. If the quality of the being was not there, it would be impossible to form a deep bond with the bare but wholesome love that dared to challenge Time.

Browning could be right after all.

Jade bent over the water, waived a finger at her reflection: "Next time, don't look for a guy who says I love you, but a man who says I want to grow old with you."

Tonight the train departed. Jade was ready. Leaving the hotel and this city behind, her steps felt lighter, for her mind was freed. She has accepted aging for what it truly was. Passengers started to gather on the platform, group by group at the doors of the train, cattle going back for a peaceful night on a familiar terrain.

Her compartment looked welcoming, warm as home. Jade turned the bed lamp on, and opened her journal.

The Bay of Childhood

Melancholy swirled with excitement as the train stopped. To revisit the place where she spent her childhood and most of her teenage summers playing in its waters was a treat and a pain to Jade.

That time of her life became a lost paradise since she grew up. She had left the haven of childhood to enter the unwelcome world of adults.

She could still find her way in this place, to all the shops along the road embracing the bay.

This bay was on the Pacific Ocean coast. The very fine sand of an off-white color, laid thick along the water blue to no end. It was the color blue of the tropical sky. Too bright, too blue, too sensual. And the melancholic eternal chant of the waves. Seas and waves did not look and sound the same. Here, waves insisted until they could pull her back to when amassed broken seashells were valued more than allowances and paychecks. They recounted stories she has forgotten since she left innocence.

Jade walked into the *Ten-year-old* store where her mother took her at the end of every summer.

Nothing looked different since Jade grew up and moved away. The same glass counter displayed all the fancy pencils in their cases, erasers of all shapes and colors, the same smell of back to school, a mix of new vinyl, plastic binders, notebooks. An imperceptible wisp of her mother's perfume came back to life when she bent over to touch a reading book. It was not back to school without that scent following all the preparations.

There were colors and there was light everywhere. There was joy hiding behind every blade of tall grass in the elementary school. There was excitement wrapping the colorful gifts whenever dad came home from his business trips. Life was full of wonderful surprises in grandmother's field on their annual visit to the countryside. Tomorrow didn't bear the weight of yesterday.

Life and happiness were much simpler. *What do I need to do, to be able to look at life the same way? To be in the state where being unhappy is the exception?*

She left the shop and walked around the bay to the Shore of Memories, to the place where her family stayed in summers.

Here it was! The big house she and her siblings used to call the Castle by the Sea. It was in fact a villa situated on top of a small hill looking out to the ocean. The rooftop had a terrace, and an alcove where nested a big bell. It was a fortress that protected the children from the storms of life.

Jade remembered ...She used to walked along the beach in the morning, collecting colorful shells, dancing kelp washed to the shore, not knowing she was collecting wonderful memories as well. In the afternoon she would have strolled in the shallow water warmed up by the sun, amazed at the scintillating golden rays that played with the blue waves. After dinner the children converged in the living room by the fireplace, to eavesdrop on adults chatting. There was no television at the castle, and no cellular phones back then. They did more things together. They were closer because they did not need man-made devices to keep their presence in each other's life.

Jade and her sister went to bed when the dark corridor to their room felt frightening. They shared the bed but silently fought for a bigger part of the blanket. Jade never won but one year, before the summer ended she got to sleep with her aunt in her full of pink and pretty things bedroom. What a victory! Because auntie Louise was mom's youngest, prettiest and nicest sister. Sometimes she spent summer with them, and when she did, that summer would be much more joyful for Jade.

In the back of the castle, on the first floor, there was a dark and big suite, quarters of the old maid. She was the housekeeper. She was always there when Jade and her family came for their annual summer vacation.

She was older than Jade's mom, and nicer: she let Jade do whatever she wanted in her space. And Jade loved to watch her boil water in a huge metal pot in the large kitchen by her bedroom. Making eau de toilette, she explained. And the recipe was a secret not to disclose to outsiders. But the old lady allowed her to help by gathering flowers which fell from enormous plumeria trees planted all around the property.

The old maid rinsed then dried them in the sun, on the sundeck right in front of the entrance to her domain, before using them in her concoction. Jade asked a lot of questions about the exciting process of making perfume. The old woman gave a lot of answers, but they were much too complicated for Jade to understand, and she did not truly care. Jade just loved to hang around her quarters because it smelled good and it felt important to be in on a secret.

Across the street lived a family with a dad a mom and a boy. The boy was one year older then she was. He told her he was nine. On the first year her family was there, she saw them on the beach. They waved and her mother went and talked to them.

The boy had a bunch of paper boats that he played with in the shallow water of the beach.

Jade ventured close to him.

He asked: "What's your name?"

"Jade."

He said: "Pretty name."

Jade tried to stop her smile from being too big.

"I'm Jimmy."

Jade knew but asked anyway: "You made the boats?"

He smiled and nodded: "Yeah."

"They're nice."

"Want it?"

Jade looked at the boy in disbelief.

"You can have it."

The boy pushed a paper boat towards Jade. Jade looked at it then glanced at him. He gave Jade a furtive look then turned and ran away. Jade picked the boat up. It was green, yellow, and red.

* * *

"Eat your breakfast, or you can't go out." Mom yelled from her room.

Breakfast was ready on the large wooden table in the kitchen. Jade finished her big plate then ran to the beach. The morning tide left the beach miles and miles in shallow water. Around well worn round boulders along the beach, water formed a pond. Jade ran to one and put the colorful boat to water. It shook but braved the wind and floated.

They talked to each other sometimes, Jade was very shy, and Jimmy's family did not go out much.

Then the next Summer Jade did not see them anymore, the old maid said they moved. Jade thought of the boy a lot in later years. The first boy who was nice to her. She wondered what happened to them, how he looked now, and if they did not move would they grow up and be very close, like boyfriend and girlfriend. Jade could make those origami boats now, many more things then a boat, but none looked as beautiful as the blue and yellow and red boat that boy made for her when she was eight.

Concrete had taken over a big part of the field by the villa. Nature was squeezed out of the developing town, trees and bushes yanked to make place for a wall. A few tufts of grass waved to the wind along the foot of the wall, reminiscence of a field that once lived there.

Jade loved fields and farms.

She ran to meet her grandma in the memories of the trips to their country house.

Once the trees and bushes stopped moving along the red dirt road to her grand parents' farm, Jade and her brothers would leap out of the car, immediately chased the wandering ducklings in the front yard. Yellow balls of fluff so soft to the touch, like Mom's special coat. Cute and tiny, they moved fast and made noise; they were warm and lively, unlike their toys.

The next morning, she went further down into the bay.

To the *Teenagers* shop.

And the teenage' years came running back! The rocky road to adulthood engendered a rocky relationship with her mother and the world. Jade was happy and miserable at the same time, for no reason. She was so happy she wished she died at the moment, she was so miserable death could not be any different. Parents were too old, too simplistic to understand the depth and sophistication of the anguish of a newer, swifter generation facing the uncertainty of their future. Parents were obsolete.

It was hip to walk on the forbidden side of life, to be rebellious: that showed that they too- her generation- had an identity. It was fun to skip studying, to hop on a train to the end of the line and wander around the station watching the hustle-bustle of goodbyes before catching the last train back.

The love that her mom had for her was too intrusive, it was not well received; plus being loved by parents was too normal; and worse, it came with rules and interdictions for living under their roof. She could not wait to grow up and get away from the watchful eyes that never seemed to close, not even in their sleep; who never saw how mature their children had become. She longed to get away from the tyranny of love and care. Great adventures were out there, waiting to be lived.

"Jade, Jaaade?" Mom's voice from the kitchen.

"Mom?" She frowned her eyebrows.

"You lather your face with too much makeup. You don't need all that thick layer of foundation. You look like you're wearing a mask. That blood lipstick is gaudy."

"I don't need your permission to wear makeup. I'm sixteen. Sixteen! Stop telling me what to do all the time." Jade yelled back from the hallway.

"Your skin is perfect at this age, why do you dust it up with powder? Where are you going?"

"Nowhere."

"Don't talk back to me. That blouse is sheer provocative. I can see your bra from here. When did you get that?"

Jade stomped into her room and slammed the door. This was why she could not wait to be a grown up. Just because they gave her monthly allowances, they thought they could enslave her.

Bits and pieces of the *hard times* ran through her tears. Jade missed having her mother trying to appeal to her common sense, looking out for her respectability and safety, the kind of notion sixteen years old found strange, useless.

Jade looked at the changing hues of the ocean, the changing hues of her emotions.

Ingratitude was what her parents received for their effort at raising their offspring to be decent people later in life. While suffering from the 'parental abuse and oppression', Jade and her siblings went to the best Catholic schools, enjoyed extended vacations while half of their friends worked at summer jobs, received monthly allowances for shopping and entertainment, private courses which they skipped.

But life intercepted. Throwing wanted and mostly unwanted adventures at her. Grown up life was not what she thought it would have been.

Her parents' company and their marriage did not survive the economic crash, a global deterioration that blew ashes on their children's future. Money became scarce. Jade started to work part time to finish college.

Facing the reality of work place and adult problems, Jade wished for the childhood in her parents' prison. Before the crash. Before the divorce. The prison that suddenly looked like a castle.

She graduated and moved. Her mother got phone calls on holidays, and she went home every other Christmas. She was busy with her life. But deep down, she knew there was a home to where she could always go back, and that certainty was the reason she took it for granted. Forgetting that the elderly mom did not live forever. Sometimes that fear brushed her thoughts, but Jade imagined she still had time.

With time and disillusions, she realized how much she needed the home of unconditional love to go back to when there was nowhere else to go, to rest in the shadow of her mother's presence, it was ripped away. Mother was not anymore, nor was the bond that tied the siblings. Change, changes. The soft lament of the waves was the sole constant. Maybe, if she looked long enough she could finally understand the message of the sea, and she might even find the answers to all questions life bears.

Her brother whom she used to fight with was not anymore, his lifespan shortened by cancer. Here she was, sitting on the beach of the younger years, picking up traces of memories hung at every corner of remembrance … tears hurried to turn cold on her cheeks.

I am sorry Mom. I love you very much and I looked up to you. I fought hard to be as successful as you were. I wished I could tell you how sorry I am for not seeing you more when you were sick. I am sorry for not being there with you in your last breaths.

Jade has hoped this visit would help her relive the time she had with her mother, and heal the wound of separation. But being here was not being back to that happy time. There was a space and time, which would never leave, that moment of happiness, unknown at the time, but so true that it carried on until the brain could no longer hold on to those memories.

It hurt to know that that time was not present anymore, that moment belonged to the past, and could not be multiplied, nor duplicated. But the pure presence of the past stayed. And the scent of those moments, the precious milestones she was lucky enough to have, lifted her heart. The hurt of their disappearance was replaced by the intense connection, the time together that death could not erase. The immortality of her loved ones.

The Alley of Broken Dreams

Jade went back to the hotel, for an escape, as crucial as it was temporary.

Families with children populated the open air restaurants, attached to all hotels that dubbed themselves resorts. A few small faces were already smeared with some kind of sauce, and dinnertime had barely begun. *Enjoy it, kids; you'll never be this carefree again. No matter how accomplished your life will be.*

To dine alone in a crowded place made Jade feel even lonelier, but the mere thought of room service for one was dreadful, and stopped her on the first step up to her room. Jade thought she found the perfect medium rarely attainable: sushi bar.

There was one in the dining room of the hotel.

The sushi bar was only half full, and Jade could snug herself in her favorite corner spot, the equivalent of the airplane window seat. Spider rolls, seared eel. *Dreamy clouds* sake, not warm, chilled.

Good food restored good mood and fresh air invited long walks. Jade left the restaurant and ventured into the comforting velvety night. Walking pass an alley, she thought she recognized it by the large knotty tree stump on one side of the curb. Yes, the Alley of Broken Dreams. It was lit by fluorescent streetlights that could not push the shadows of distress away.

As if she was approaching her dream, and not wanting to wake it up for she might break it, Jade made a few steps forward, and stood there for a long moment. Then curious, she entered.

A face emerged from the dark of a forgotten past, Pierre. Jade crossed her arms, touching her shoulders. She saw the coat he put over her shoulders on their first night out. Not wanting to cover the sexy dress she ended up in a chilly night with a strapless frock without a jacket. Stupid things done for the hope of love.

When he pulled her in, she looked into his eyes, and fell into the dark deep blue enveloping ocean's bottom. When he kissed her, she realized the pull of gravity had bound her all her life. She clung to him, savoring the flight.

But the feeling was too strong, she was scared of losing herself, and started to sabotage their relationship. Why Pierre was not more spiritual? He would be perfect if he was. He lived in a city by the sea, and she in a city surrounded by mountains. Distance could be a problem, although Jade always loved the sea, and believed if he was the right guy, it would be the right move. And so on. She broke up with him without an explanation. Was it Fate, whatever that meant, to be blamed? Jade might never know why, only that she regretted it. The poignant truth was much more simple, she was plain stupid. When stupidity interfered, consequences were coming. He did not pick up the phone when she tried to make up. And life put distance in their closeness, and her pride took over.

After college, marriage and divorce, Pierre was still single. If and if made sure that the old times never came back. But the short moment they knew each other stayed present in the aching regret and the surge of untamed tenderness that warmed her body up at the mere thought of him.

His train passed by, she caught a glimpse of what could have been but it was impossible for it to materialize now. *Could we be on the same train, experience life on the same timeline? We had loved each other, yet we watched each other disappear from each other's life.*

Penetrating the dark, Jade found an old handbag that looked as if it was the corpse of a cat. The bag contained the deep envy of her friend's talent, whose art was widely appreciated. An artist who made a great living was a success Jade envied. She did take all the courses needed, and thought of herself as artistic, but deep down she knew something was missing, that spark of talent she desperately told herself she had but reality belied.

Scattered on a bench were the remains of another dream. The dream of having a different life, that family's money still abounded, and her parents got back together.

All her childhood friends, she wondered how they were doing, what path their life had taken, were they happy, were they miserable, did they attain their younger years dreams? Or have they become the youth of darkness, with no identity, no flavor, followers of the day's fad?

Shards of the dream of changing the world scattered on the street, the dream which was trampled by the very world she wanted to help. The big dream now reduced to changing herself, and applauding the accomplishment of others without bitterness. And there were illusions of success. And there were failures disguised as acceptance.

Jade had walked straight into the dark of shattered dreams.

She volunteered at a prison every Sunday. After the session, on the way out passing by the lobby, she saw the same faces week after week, waiting to get in the visiting room. When they caught her eyes, they shifted uncomfortably on the metal chairs, as if they tried to take up less space.

The families of the inmates, patiently held the look of disdain society threw on them, guilty by association, week after week came back to the concrete hell to visit their loved ones. Jade believed the prisoners' family knew quite well what put them there, but the inextinguishable love and support for the prisoners did not stem from approbation of their acts, but from the memories of the kids they once were. The love for the children who were loving, angelic, those memories that would not die or change nor be erased. They looked with the secret eyes that saw those children live, albeit secretly, in the adults whose innocence has dried up.

It was easy to like good karma, it was easy to like nice people and good deeds. It was not so easy to like the consequences of bad actions, of our own or others. And yet, these family members were there, rain or shine, to assuage their own need of closeness, to live life in the moment. And the bond that tied those who were lost to those who were grounded was the boat that brought hope home, and blew new dreams into those lost lives trapped in the unforgiving barbwire world. Dreams of redemption.

Pieces of broken dreams formed the layers of nacre that enwrapped the grain of sand, of dust, of discomfort at the heart of a pearl. It started with pain and ended in beauty. If dreams did not die, hope could not live, for hope lived on broken dreams, and with their remnants started a fire to light a new one.

Tears of those broken dreams softened and watered the heart for its growth, tears were not to be feared after all.

Tomorrow she would travel to a different place. In the morning she would walk to the train station, and from afar she could make the shiny black body of the train, the body of a giant snake waiting in the sun, blowing its impatience into short strident whistles, as it was impossible to delay the black conductor of Karma. Tomorrow, the train would take her to another city, into another uncertain world.

But tonight, she could gather all the warm memories of childhood, all the dreams that her trusting self had dared, broken as they were, and make a comfortable bed for her to lie down upon and build newer ones. Dreams did not die, they only shifted their shape.

The City of Words

Jade did not have to look very long for Yvonne. After she crossed the gate of the train station, her attention was immediately drawn to the bordeaux convertible parked provocatively by the curb on the right side. A woman in her thirties leaned against the door in a yellow dress that brightened her face, her grin, and the afternoon around her.

Jade had spent three years studying in this city, had met Yvonne, and they became friends for life. Not seeing each other for years, their mail still spilled affection that did not feel the distance, time or space.

"I hope I have enough room for your

suitcases." Yvonne said as they hugged.

Jade looked at the trident emblem and forced a face she thought read evil, but she ruined it with a frank grin.

"When did you get this ugly ride?"

"Oh! It's been a couple of years."

"Just looking at the color makes me drunk."

Her friend smiled: "That's how you should be the entire time staying here."

The trunk had more room then it looked, accommodated the suitcases fine. They got in and Jade inclined her chair back, made herself comfortable.

"I wish I understood art. I'd be living a life of leisure with sports cars."

Yvonne said: "You know that there is a huge element of luck and Ben's contribution as well."

Jade "How is he?"

"Doing fine. He said he's sorry he's not home to visit with you. Architect convention." Her right hand left the wheel to tap Jade's left arm. "We have all the time for ourselves."

Jade grinned, but dutifully added: "Your husband is a nice man. Sorry you have to stay home for me."

"I wouldn't miss this for the world. It's been ages since we've seen each other at your…" Yvonne wanted to say wedding, but stopped herself in time. It was a fresh wound and any reminder would make it bleed.

As Yvonne drove, they tried to relay to each other all the events in their respective lives, although in words they sounded flat, something one read in papers with chuckles and exclamations but no emotional connection.

The wrought iron gate opened to the long river rock driveway. It curved in front of a construction that gave brick and mortar a soul. Yvonne stopped the car by the front steps.

"Very beautiful." Jade said.

"Thanks. Ben designed it and we worked on it for two years. Let's get the suitcases to your room."

Yvonne led Jade to the side of the mansion

where an opening housed the marble stairs to the upper level. She stopped in front of an oak door on the left at the end of the staircase. A cast iron bell hung on the side of the door, the leather cord softened the severe look of the square bell.

She opened the door: "Hope you like this room."

Jade did not say anything. She was not able to, busy at controlling her reaction. It was not a room, it was a suite. The floor was wooden. Not any wood, the pattern of deep brown to charcoal black stripes on cream to pale lemon was one of the best of nature's art. It was set against the white walls and the square bed's white linen in the middle. The painted serene sky opened the high ceiling to infinite height. A single oil painting hung on the wall. Probably signed Yvonne T. for Yvonne Tillens, Jade recognized the brushwork. One wall was all glass, showcased an alcove with a table and two chairs, its backdrop was the stone wall that encircled the property. On the wall were carvings of figures in different meditative positions.

Finally Jade found her voice in a whisper: "This is gorgeous. No, not gorgeous. The carvings are breathtaking."

"I like to wake up to a peaceful face. Then after my coffee, the turmoil can begin."

"Your piece?"

"I drew them and had them carved by stone workers in South-East Asia and shipped here. I hand picked the slabs."

"They look more art than craftsmanship."

"I did some finishing touches. Obligation towards my nitpicking personality."

"Did you kill the last rain forest for this zebrawood floor?"

Yvonne's shoulders hunched and chased her smile away. She said softly: "This is one thing that I regret."

Jade hurried, "I'm sorry. I have a macabre sense of humor. But you know that."

"I should have used other wood but I loved the look of this zebra so much I could not resist."

After the suitcases were properly stored in the walk-in closet the size of a normal bedroom, Yvonne took Jade on a tour of her property. The same solid zebrawood planks covered both floors of the mansion. Furniture and decoration were kept to a minimum to set off the exotic look of the wood, while all the ceilings were painted and the walls almost bare. The design gave a feel of openness rarely experienced inside a home.

The landscape was distinctly divided in two parts by vegetation. The rock garden closer to the house had a large pond populated by lively kois. Red and black lava rocks covered the ground, boulders placed at random and tuffs of hardy exotic plants grew around them broke up the monotony of the landscape. The perimeter was assorted greenery bordered by tall maples. Looking from the rock garden, it evoked disbelief and hope, as did a mirage in the desert. Yvonne's studio was built in that land of dreams. And a network of paths in the garden were covered by cedar wood planks.

Jade fell half asleep when she finally got back to her room; she slumped on the bed in exhaustion, a faint attempt to get to the bath was crushed by heavy eyelids.

"Get dressed, we're going to dinner." The cattle bell and the yelling awoke Jade from her slumber. She tried to sit up as Yvonne kept ringing and yelling.

Nightfall already?

"All right. I need a bath and time to get ready."

"Of course. One hour."

The night was warm, the company warmer. Food and wine combination was known to spark great conversation, or wild assumption.

Jade: "Ah. The beauty of night. The beauty of silence."

"Beauty is also in words. In literature." Yvonne said.

"Beauty exists before words. In unstructured utterance." Jade countered.

Yvonne shrugged: "Not well expressed nor refined."

Jade: "Sounds are universal, that's why music speaks to all beyond languages."

Yvonne: "Agree. That's thoughts orchestrated in sounds."

Jade added: "And gestures, moves."

Yvonne said: "Dance. Structure and refinement."

Jade looked at her: "That depends. Ballet is affected."

Yvonne: "No, rules are the necessary purification process in order to attain a certain effect."

Jade: "That is saying go through hell to find heaven. Art is an imitation of life that calls itself unique. No offense."

Yvonne raised her eyebrows: "One taken. Order is the ... Are you advocating chaos?"

"I think going through all possible combinations to find the best for self is good, but it's still arbitrary. Tainted truth. Why are you scared of chaos? For chaos to exist, it has to have some order to it. The order of no order."

Jade sipped her wine and continued: "Purification creates class. Class creates problems."

"Class difference is something you can't deny nor erase."

"Hmm".

Jade ran her eyes over the room to stall and avoid the discussion. A couple at a table by them suddenly stopped talking.

Her friend asked: "How's work?"

Jade sighed: "The same killjoys. People think that women stick together in all matters. Assumption and generalization equals wrong."

After a pause, she added: "*L'enfer c'est les autres*". Hell is the others, viva Sartre".

Yvonne shook her head: "L'enfer c'est soi-même. Hell is yourself. *The others* exist because you let them in. But I think above competition at the work place, the VIC factor makes it worse for you."

"The VIC factor?" Jade asked, eyes wide.

"Vagina Identity Crisis. It happens when a woman feels threatened by another woman without provocation and acts upon her imagination."

Jade smiled," That crisis hits me sometimes."

"No. It doesn't. Everybody has felt envious of others, but it's not the same as lashing out from vicious jealousy. And that's class difference, on a minimal scale. Those women set us back a hundred year. Subconsciously or consciously they value themselves through men's attention."

"Some people would call you anti-feminist".

"Then they're still fighting their gender war, not I. If they can't honestly admit to a person's shortcomings because of her gender, then the issue is with them". Yvonne raised her glass, toasting her victory.

"What about guys who behave like assholes right off the bat?"

"Those men have SPS, forget them. Actually, you should feel sorry for sick people."

"What is SPS?"

"Small Penis Syndrome."

Jade laughed, "*Ivanne* the Terrible!"

Yvonne prompted: "Check your historical facts, Ms. It's *Ivanne* the Wise."

Jade looked at her friend, still shaken by laughter, wondering if she would ever have that assurance in dealing with people.

The days were filled with shopping bags and visits to art galleries, food experiences to conversations and reading in the woods when Yvonne worked. The pavilion which Yvonne used as a studio had painted brick walls, high ceiling and exposed wood beams. Jade loved the look, the interior, and the content: Yvonne's paintings. It was a world inaccessible to her. What colors and shapes could convey in seconds needed hundreds of words.

"The paintings are up for adoption", that was how Yvonne let Jade know about her upcoming exhibition. The buyers paid for the privilege of hanging her art in their home, or wherever they liked, but for Yvonne, it was and would always be her child. A piece of her heart followed that child to wherever it went.

Jade said with surprise: "I don't see The Muse."

"That was adopted two months ago."

"Oh." There was so much disappointment in Jade's tone that Yvonne stopped arranging the brushes to look at her, something in Yvonne's eyes looked like remorse.

Jade fell in love with that painting the first time she saw it. A river ran through a land of nightmarish colors and forms then ended as an androgynous being with perfect breasts. The big head had flowing hair that reached a sun. The eyes were immensely calm and sad. The oil painting shocked the viewers with the contrasting glorious sun and dark landscape, an easy feeling of joy and despair at once. The beauty and profound expression of the eyes fought with the

108

natural attention drawn to the very carnal painted breasts. Jade was not sure if she understood the artist, but it drew and immersed her in a fright and delight at the same time, made her face her deep, intimate feelings in a most uncomfortable way. The anguish of being on this side of the fence longing for the other, while fully aware what Self did to Self.

Jade reveled in the luxurious stay, enjoyed every single detail that made the days comfortably beautiful and the nights beautifully comfortable. But at the same time, she felt like a stranger in Alice's Wonderland. She kept telling herself this is the Yvonne I've known all my life, yet her friend's success separated them into two worlds.

Money created distance. Here was where Yvonne bought her household items; there was where Jade shopped. Here was where she got her shoes and purses, and there was Jade's favorite discount store ... Although the difference did not affect their friendship, it created a well of things they did not have in common. Superficial? The well was deep. Did things define who they were? Since when were things allowed to take control?

I shop here because I do not have good taste, you shop there means you are classy, not because you can afford something nicer but overtly overpriced. Is every act of consumerism transcended into some cultural meaning or translated into some clue into your psyche?

People defined themselves by the things they bought. The thought of that paid identity made her stomach churn. Being wealthy is relative. Jade is wealthy compared to a person living in a hut doing manual work for food. Beyond the basic needs, money comes back to the perception of Self or perceptions of others about Self. Money is Ego.

Her ego bruised because she lacked the buying power. Talent and luck, who decided who would get that and who would not? And herself, why split hairs in fourths?

Next morning over breakfast, Yvonne said:

"I'm thinking about taking you sight seeing to a chateau. About four hours drive from here. It's in a small village where I often take my easel. The village formed around the chateau decades after decades. The backside of the chateau is a cliff. But that's not why I ask you to visit the place."

" There is icing on the cake?" Jade asked.

"Yes. The chateau belongs to a family that doesn't live there, and it's a historic site open to the public. But there are rumors." Yvonne drawled.

"What are the rumors?" Jade's interest piqued.

"People hear noises, sometimes lights at night."

"The caretaker?" Jade asked.

"Nobody lives in the chateau. The caretaker is a villager, he does the cleaning during daytime then goes home." Yvonne replied.

"Interesting."

"Scared?" Yvonne looked at Jade, trying to read her friend's facial expression.

"No. But your point?" Jade rolled her eyes.

"Do you want to visit it at night?"

"How do we get in? We camp outside?"

"I have the keys. The owners are my friends. I go there to sketch sometimes, didn't see anything unusual. But I didn't stay overnight. We'll spend the night to see if the rumors have foundations."

It did not take much more to intrigue Jade. Not knowing what to expect, the mystery was a strong spirited drink mixed with the exotic flavor of anticipation; it could get her drunk all the way to the time of departure for the adventure.

The afternoon was noisy with preparations. To-and-fro for snacks, flashlights, water, insect repellant, the usual props. Yvonne took her backpack to the garage where three cars slept and opened the trunk of the Italian.

"You're taking this car?" Jade asked.

"Yes. Why?" Yvonne looked at her.

"I thought you would want less risk of damage and low mileage with this car?" Jade replied.

"I'm no nouveau riche. And that sounds like 'You can enjoy foreplay but you're not allowed to cum'."

Jade laughed: "Did you really say that?"

They drove to the village at the time when the day's activities have cooled down and the night's enthusiasm was still dormant. Smaller houses fenced with hedges and bushes replaced cold walled citadels as the roads got smaller and the sky larger. After two or three CDs of old love songs and bedroom anecdotes, the village appeared in the view, a clump of red tiled roofs at the foot of a small hill.

They drove on the main road that cut through the village; flashes of brightly painted doors and shutters went by in the parsimonious streetlights. The road led them to a parking area at the foot of the hill, where the chateau looked down the village and its inhabitants from a cliff. The way to the castle was wide enough for a car to pass, but Jade could make out the steps from her seat. They would have to hike.

A few lanterns dangled in the night breeze on a post at the entrance of the way.

"It is not very far up, Jade." Yvonne encouraged.

They strapped on their backpacks and half way up, Jade saw the door. The iron details on barn wood looked ancient and discouraging at the same time. The ornate plaque around the keyhole was rusty, the imposing size of the door was menacing. It seemed to say '*Do not approach*'.

Yvonne put her backpack down and unzipped its side pocket. She exhibited an abnormally large black key, put it in the keyhole, turned, grounded her feet and leaned forward to push on the door.

"Flashlight over here Jade."

Jade directed the beam at Yvonne, who turned on the switch, and the benevolent light from the chandelier in the middle of the hall fell upon them, casting aside the thick darkness and the rising discomfort.

They looked each other, and Jade asked:

"Where did people see light? This light? And the noise, from where?"

Then an eerie sensation filled the hall as the light flickered, but it came back almost instantly. The high ceiling, the marble floor with dark veins ran on grayish white did not spell a warm welcome. And the imposing stairs took the eyes to mysterious rooms behind the alcove above the hall added a sinister note.

Yvonne pointed to a range of doors on the right:

"The bedrooms are on this side, and more upstairs. People saw balls of light chasing each other in here, and heard noises, but nobody came close enough to know what it was. We can sleep in there and if either of us hears anything strange, we'll wake each other up. Unless you want to stand guard all night?"

"I'd rather rest and see what happens."

"Let's do that."

Jade fell exhausted and wanted to retreat to her bed.

"Goodnight Yve."

"Night Jadie."

Jade opened the door that Yvonne pointed out and stepped inside. The caretaker proved that he earned his keep. Anything and everything that was brass shone in the dimly lit bedroom.

Jade looked around. The bed was in the center, quite small for the room, and its carved wooden headboard gave out an uncomfortable last century feel. A sofa and a loveseat sprawled by the only window that ran almost the height of the wall, their golden taupe and garnet red brocade upholstery evoked the splendor of the past. In front of the fireplace a large chair and a small table completed the idea of yesteryears' comfort. She sat her backpack and her tired body on the sofa and began to take off her shoes.

What did people see here? What kind of noise?

Suddenly the walls seemed to move back. Jade stopped unlacing her right shoe.

She saw Words in different colors running in all directions; and the walls were covered with them. Some Words were stashed in the corners, Words that looked old and wrinkled, hidden or forgotten. Shyness' blue halo lit up a corner when Jade pulled it out from behind the window's drape. Some were buried, but their fire, like gems' fire, blasted through the ashes in the firebox. Love in intense red was half-covered. Integrity in dark blue and Hope in tender green dangled on the mantelpiece. Words danced all around rendering her speechless. This feeling would need a thousand words, uttered at the same time, to accurately describe it, hence silence. Silence was the best choice of word. Silence was full of soundless screams.

The air felt thicker, and her head lighter.

Words hid under the sofas, in the drawers, jumped out at her when she looked at them. It seemed that Jade was lost in a World of Words, a labyrinth with no Ariadne's thread to give any hope of escaping. She thought of running for the door, Words attacked her. She thought of calling out for Yvonne, Words jumped in her mouth. They flew everywhere, angrily, disturbed by her unwanted

116

presence. They hit her and Jade fell to the ground, unconscious. When she came around, Words sentenced themselves up in glistening lines, circled her like prey. Then their light turned threatening, screamingly bright. 'Wasting words,' the sentence read. 'Use words as the truth parallel.' 'Masquerade of truth in a dance of words', on the right side of the window. 'Use words to drown thoughts', on the left. Jade felt a cold sword piercing her heart with every word she read, when suddenly they started to talk. The mechanical voice trailed and made her gasp.

"Why are you here?"

"What are you?" Her trembling words struggled to be audible.

"You know. Why ask when you already know? We're Words."

"But … You SPEAK." *This is a nightmare, I'll wake up soon.*

"Of course we speak, because we exist. We are the accumulation of genuine feelings and have lived through the ages, as ancient as your ancestors. We are not invisible. We are not weightless. But you abuse us without shame. You use us to lie for you. You use us as if we have no dignity, just cleaning rags put at your disposition. 'Use them, abuse them, there will be no consequence.' Well, there Is."

"I am sorry." Jade mumbled.

"That doesn't erase what you did." Clear and cutting reply.

"I'll be careful, I didn't know."

"You did not know what? That what you've done to us would not be known?"

Jade blinked, the sweat on her forehead dripped into her eyes.

"When you don't respect us, you disrespect yourself." Even in the state that she was in, Jade had to agree.

Pause, then it continued: "Do not waste Words. Use Words like using a knife: with intention, precise, not a single superfluous move."

"I promise."

"Promise?" Could sarcasm be detected in a mechanical voice, or did her paranoia take over? "Promise has a shelf life. How long is yours?"

"I'll do it right away." Jade tried.

"With every word that you use, every time you

118

talk?" Now there was insistence in the voice.

"I cannot always be that alert, that mindful, but I promise ... to be diligent about it."

"Another promise?"

No answer.

"Shorten your promises. Use Words to expand thoughts, not to dilute them. One more thing, we see you, we hear you. Every one of us used by you is remembered. You will pay for how you use us."

"How ... what kind of consequences?"

"Typical of you people. You want to know the consequences before choosing a course of action instead of deciding to be decent from the start."

Jade heard her breath precipitate and her heartbeat in her ears. She forced herself to exhale slowly, then asked:

"Are you what you represent? Are you Hate? Are you Love?"

"We are the boat. We are the bridge. You are the person who does the crossing."

Jade felt her nails in her palms. Fear propelled

her up on shaky legs, and she bolted ahead. Jade ran and ran. She might get away before they rounded her up again. But she ended up in the same room, between the same walls.

Yvonne found Jade on the floor of the hall in the morning. She ran to her friend, at the same time that Jade woke up. She helped her friend up, tried to look in her eyes to check for concussion.

"Are you hurt? Were you on the floor all night?"

"I think so."

"Oh! How come? What happened? I saw you go into the bedroom."

"I did. I might have come out and fallen asleep here, on the floor."

"Why? I didn't hear anything unusual. Did you hear or see something that made you come out? Why didn't you call me?"

Jade was totally awake now. She remembered last night when she tried to escape but seemed to be circling the bedroom. After that, what happened? Why did she end up in the hall?

"No. I did not see anything." She could not afford to tell Yvonne about what had happened. It could also be a dream. It could be that her imagination lived out its fantasy. She should not give Yvonne a reason to worry about her.

She asked softly: "Did you see or hear anything?"

"No. I actually had a very good sleep."

"We should head back."

Yvonne yawned and proposed: "Breakfast?"

"Not hungry. I'd like to go back, clean up, then have some of your awesome coffee first." Jade caught her breath and looked around sheepishly. She has used words to hide the truth.

"I'm not terribly hungry either but are you sure you don't want to look around, visit the place? The back of this castle looks down an abrupt cliff where waves crash at its feet. A real fortress. The village has some very good eateries. All home made, no bland chain-restaurant food here. But no awesome coffee either."

Jade shook her head, "I think I'll pass."

"This is not like you. Are you all right?"

Jade thought she should say something to deflect the suspicion that might have taken roots in her friend's observing mind. Normally she would sniff around a new place and take in the experience with all her senses, and Yvonne knew that. *I slept on the floor all night. My back feels funny. It misses the mattress.* That would be another lie, albeit innocent but still a lie.

Last night definitely was not a dream. She desperately wanted to leave this place, this village, and her shaken self. Suddenly it struck her that Words spoke to her in a language she could understand, what if …? *When we talked, isn't it words that take control, rather than thoughts?*

In the world empty of thoughts animated by words, who's doing the talking?

"I know I'm not myself. I'm very tired. Too tired to appreciate the beauty of this area. Probably because I was on the floor all night."

The drive home was heavy with untold words and lurking thoughts. Yvonne looked pensive, and Jade constrained. She knew she was not fair to her friend: "Hey, I'm sorry. I have a lot on my mind. Thank you for taking me here. I loved the journey to the Blue Beard castle."

Yvonne burst out laughing. There was relief in the way Yvonne's joyful laughter rang out and in Jade's discreet sigh.

"That chateau does look secret and spooky, doesn't it?" Yvonne admitted.

The conversation came back quickly as time flew by the car's window. It seemed to reverse with the scenery showing in the opposite order.

They had breakfast at Yvonne's favorite café, and Jade's, too, as she came to know it. The tiny place coyly sat on a side street, away from the other restaurants on the main road. The ones full of chrome and glass and useless porch lights with models disguised as servers but strutting about with that runway attitude.

In this cozy kitchenette, the owner who was also the chef decided the menu for the customers and the customers, without exception, loved it. Was it the art of judging people by the look down to a psychic power, knowing what they would like, or was he simply a spectacular cook?

Yvonne pushed the glass door and the bell over the door rang *Hungry, hungry…*

"Good morning ladies. Good to see you, Yvonne". The chef greeted them from his kingdom, behind the half wall separating the kitchen and the small dining area. It was late for the first meal of the day, but all the tables were taken.

"Good morning, Joe." Yvonne responded.

A host came with a smiled: "There is a 20 minute wait, will that be all right?"

"That's fine." Yvonne said. "I'm happy we even have a table."

Finally, they could take possession of the first available table, situated in the middle of the room. Then it did not take long for the food to come. The friends' eyes were on the server when he walked towards them, in his hands the reward for their patience, a promising tray! Two large identical plates, with what Joe felt like cooking today. Portabellas in their full glorious sun shape rested on a green sky of mixed herbs and strings of what looked like ginger. Toasted crisp artisan bread. Asparagus and bacon quiches added a creamy touch.

Only ten minutes into the savory meal, Jade picked up the train of thought:

"Let's imagine an artist, a writer who can't communicate, talk or write his thoughts down, anymore. Is his artistic sense or genius less because it's unexpressed?"

Her friend answered: "No. But it's not noticed because art is the expression, the communication of his mind, or heart, as you like."

Jade: "The power of expression that moves; but without the source, there will be no expression."

Yvonne argued: "Of course. But genius also lies in the way that inner source flows out. I don't doubt or question the artistic sense, my judgment lies on the use of the medium. In fact, he's not even a writer or artist anymore because he's not defending his name.

"Judging what is not there is not wise." Jade insisted.

"You are being circular, Jade." Yvonne ended the remark with the last piece of mushroom and an erotic grunt normally saved for the bedroom.

Jade reprised: "The source of the expression is present, the expression can be anything."

Yvonne said: "If that expression is soundless,

wordless, how can I possibly understand the artist? Hence it's not my fault if he's not recognized. You can't expect people to read his mind, or do the work for him. How can he be called an artist or a writer in the first place?"

"He still is, but not called by that name, not labeled."

Jade drank her cup then measured her words: "Do you remember the story of an obscure artist who kissed a blank canvas of a famous artist and was charged with destroying or damaging a work of art?"

"Oh yes. Phaedrus. Avignon 2007." Yvonne said.

Jade continued, "A blank canvas was accepted as art. Plato's Phaedrus becomes that artist's Phaedrus. The conversation between Socrates and Phaedrus was drawn into infinity by the virgin canvas that expresses the purity of truth, and interpreted, well, understood as such. Why couldn't a blank book?"

Yvonne: "That artist is known for his style, his expressions. That understanding and acceptance of his originality sets the stage for the interpretation of this piece. If he had nothing else to assert his talent, probably his Phaedrus would be viewed very

126

differently. And that lady, the kisser, disrupted the stream of consciousness of his art."

"That proved my point, we don't need expressions or words." Jade said triumphantly.

"You must remember that his work has a close relationship with words. But I guess you can absolutely skip words and still be able to communicate the essential. By the same token, you can communicate lies and incapacity too.

As in having no talent and not being exposed." Yvonne paused to let the remark sink in. "We live in a dimensional world. It needs tangible proof to base an opinion upon."

Jade persisted: "We can also use words to debate facts. By the way, how many Shakespeares did the world not recognize because they wrote in the wrong language? Imagine Gitanjali was not translated into English. Would we have ever known that Tagore existed?"

"There is Art, the communication in colors and forms."

"Writing is the Art of Words. Words are paper money that only has value if it has truth as backing. If the truth is untold, is it devalued? Is it still truth?"

"A truth untold is a truth unknown. Unrecognized."

"A truth untold is a truth unchanged."

"Jade, I didn't know you're that cynical" said Yvonne jokingly. "Live and learn."

The repartee was swift, "Never too late. Anyway, an untold truth stays as it is. In its prenatal state."

Yvonne brought her cup to her lips and observed her friend. Jade talked with animation, passionate in debate as she always was, argument built around a fixed point in her head. Her brown eyes were almost amber in the bright day, drifting, as if they were following an invisible point in space; the facial muscles seemed strained. Yvonne realized all her talking was the by-product of something else that was bothering her.

Jade went on like there was no tomorrow: "Words are free, because languages are the common heritage of humanity. They are valuable, but free to use. We should show gratitude by having the decency to use them sparingly, rightly, well. They are a currency, and the richest are not always the purest."

Yvonne: "What did that castle do to you?"

Jade knew how sharp and observing Yvonne was and the experience at the chateau was dancing on her lips ready to sprint out. She looked at her friend, trendy in her blue sequin top and factory worn, supposedly low key jeans, both arms on the table leaning over towards her, sparks of intelligence in the eyes; behind Yvonne she saw the bright day outside the bay window and happy faces of passers by; she heard the doorbell ring and Joe's greeting; the sound of silverware rattling as the waiter cleaned up the table by their side.

Last night, I met Words. They materialized and they talked to me. They warned me about …

Saying this would be That awkward moment when a friend you thought you knew told you she was abducted by aliens. Yvonne might believe her, but Jade would rather avoid the risk of ridicule. Words on her lips rolled down the throat with saliva and the smile went to the waiter: "May I have the check?" And turned to her friend "Let me get this. My turn."

In the afternoon, Yvonne retreated to her studio. Jade knew she did not welcome visitors when she was at work, nor did Jade want to disturb. In fact she was happy with this alone time to sort out the event of last night, and a ride to the woods would be good for her balance. She took the bike from the hangar and rode to her sanity.

Jade got off the bike and walked with it on the dirt path covered in rotten leaves. She saw the Lady-in-White standing at a clearing ahead, sunlight played on her dress. Jade looked at the friendly expression and started to cry, not knowing why. Then she told her about the encounter in the castle.

The Lady-in-White said: "You did not hallucinate, words are as old as the human species, of course they have accumulated some form of life and power. They are the measure of time."

Jade asked: "Why did I see them and Yvonne did not?"

The lady answered: "Only people who are open to sounds, who have an affinity with sound can see and hear them."

"But I'm no musician. I'm tone deaf."

"You can hear beyond words. You sense."

They followed the dirt path that led deeper into the woods, under the filtered greenish sunlight, the muffled sound of their steps, their sole lively companion.

Jade asked again: "Do words die, since they have birth?"

The Lady-in-White stepped aside to avoid a branch hanging low over the path then answered: "They do, words that are not in tandem with the newer culture and society become obsolete and when unused, they die. New needs engender new words. Words are covers, so they die. Sounds don't die because they are the voice of unnamed truth. Unless nothing exists, sounds will always be. Words are free but there is a catch; their shadows are responsibility. When you lift a word, responsibility is its reverse. And do you know what stalks responsibility? Consequences."

Jade looked at her companion: "To be mindful of words use, do I say hate when I hate? The repercussions will not be good."

"When you hate, you have said it in many other ways, from your thoughts emanate the sounds that your lips haven't done. No need to be louder than necessary. But hate is hurtful to yourself because the energy of hate gets to you first."

Jade lowered her voice: "And when I love?"

"If you wore Love in your being, you do not need to utter it. Then when you must say it, it has the contingent palpability that makes the word meaningful. If you carried compassion in your heart, every sound you make would have the echo of compassion. On the other hand, some words are sacred places. They take the listeners to a different plane, where the simple brush with them opens into infinity. They're called mantras. Intention colors each word and changes its intrinsic value, its intended meaning."

"I used to love words, now I'm scared of their sound. The responsibility attached to them is more than their worth." Jade said, regret in her voice.

"If they have the power to move then I'd say those words are priceless." The lady replied.

They went deeper into the woods, the thick silence was broken with sounds less identifiable.

"Word and sound, which one is more powerful?" Jade was startled by her own voice.

The Lady-in-White said: "Sound is the voice of word. Word is the sound of thought. Sound is uttered emotion, the primal expression that exists before word. Sound is the earliest, deepest, truest state of self-recognition. And your thought has sound. That sound has a different wavelength and thus appears soundless to you because your ears can't catch it. Any movement, as in thinking, to acting, sends a ripple of sounds into the universe."

Jade had more questions: "Does that mean sound is more powerful?"

Answer: "Sounds come before words. I do not need to hear the words you speak, I can hear the sound your heart makes when your thought starts. The sound of joy or hurt, bitterness or sweetness, anger or forgiveness. If you listen to sounds, not words or languages, you'll see how beautiful each phoneme, each breath is. And it's all music. The music of the Angry, the music of the Sage, the music of the Lover, the music of the World. You know that hate is fleeting, or joy is fugacious, and reach the deep serenity where all sounds converge and sleep in its unbroken peace".

The dirt path was over grown with shrubs and ferns in gradation of greens. Trees extended their branches in sleeves of moss to grab the handlebars, attempting to stop the intruder.

Jade struggled to get the bike to go straight. It swerved and stopped at times, refusing to venture where it couldn't run free. Her companion walked by her side with ease, as if the woods had not tried to bother her. The path suddenly widened as ferns halted their invasion and retreated to the feet of the large trees. Not far ahead, light came down in oblique streams, another glade was in view.

The Lady-in-White continued: "Don't listen to the surface of words, listen to the underlying truth. Then you'll hear that all beings have the same cry of pain when hurt, hear their same cry of joy when happy, hear the same cry of fear when afraid. You are equal in pain and in joy. That's the equanimity of life, the cosmic law. The cry of pain doesn't taint itself with race, the cry of joy doesn't distinct itself with color".

They arrived at the clearing as she talked, her white dress immersed in the dying light of day.

"This universe has never been quiet. There always are some sounds: the sound of your blood running through your veins, the molecules moving in your body, the forming of atoms in matter. Thoughts have sounds. Thoughts make sounds. Beware of this bustling world and beware of your thoughts."

Jade asked: "How do I practice listening?"

"Imagine you're pouring oil into water and listening, not only with your hearing, but with all

134

your senses, to the sound that it would make."

Jade pondered the thought for a while, then asked: "If the universe has never been quiet, then how do I rest?"

"Rest in compassion."

Jade looked at the leaves at her feet, rotten by moisture yet the early autumn vivid red appeared in the kaleidoscope of browns. She lowered her voice: "Will you travel to my next city? Will I see you again?"

The Lady-in-White's eyes searched for hers, and Jade thought she could hear 'Of course, I am where you are.'

* * *

Jade sat at the table in the balcony admiring the faces on the stone wall. Under the moon's bluish luminescence, the carvings looked mysterious and alive. Night was an excuse for art lighting in Yvonne's gardens.

Oh night, immense night, how many mysteries slept under your soft cover?

She was no longer upset by the strange confrontation in the chateau. Being denied existence and respect would cause anybody, anything to be vocal; in fact, she was grateful for the encounter. She understood words better.

Accepted as reliable conductors, words represent thoughts, and draw their power from the symbolism. But sometimes words are afraid of the emotions they were named after, they hide. When the sentiment is stronger than the word, too heavy to convene, words were ashamed of their incapacity and preferred to cover themselves in the notorious blank veil. When words were hollow, they flew out easier, they flew out more.

Words can kill, words can heal. Words are round with thoughts filled with meaning and shined with intention. Words could be flat with emptiness of the user's soul. The most powerful thing in the world is free.

She could mentally edit a conglomeration of words that left the mouth of people she knew, people whom found the sound of their voice delectable and their choice of words phenomenal. And mentally edited the writing intending to be intellectual, to be interesting. The lame wordsmiths who murdered her muse with their pens. Write to be genuine was the hardest thing to do, and going down into the center of self was not an adventure that anyone could undertake. Some people should leave words alone. Infusing new uses to old words, sometimes they created a Frankenstein of syntax.

Jade felt she could no longer abuse, 'borrow' words the way she did, now that she knew the burden of responsibility come with their usage.

I love words, I don't want to use words to hide my stupidity, my shallowness, my incompetence.

In the last moonlit night in this city, Jade was content that she could make peace with Words. That she could see her shortcoming and avoid antagonizing the invisible army.

Morning hurried inside. The house woke up with the friends' footsteps and chatter. Suitcases packed, breakfast eaten, Yvonne pulled the car into the driveway. She put the suitcases in the trunk, while Jade put both their purses in the backseat. The drive to the train station was too fast, the road too short, the memories too long.

"Au revoir, Jadie." Yvonne choked on her words.

"Good bye. I'll write you."

"I'll send you the pictures. Call me when you're home."

"I will. Bye."

Jade looked away. Goodbye, a word that sounded sad on its own, before any attached meaning. She did not know when she would see her friend again, it could be next summer, if Yvonne could come, or if she could take off. If.

The embrace lingered, then it was time. Jade hated goodbyes.

The City of Dogmas

The whistle woke the sleepy train. Another city slowly approached. The train's wheels screeched on the rails calling for passengers who poured out of their compartment doors, talking and laughing. Jade looked at the city's blue welcoming sign as the train slid into the station, "Welcome to Dogma City" and could not help a skeptical smile. Too many dogmas resulted in the robotification and demoralization of individuality.

Jade did not like to involve God in her misfortunes, her weaknesses, or her behavior. The strongest ally anyone could have was the truth. If the truth was on one's side, then one did not need to bring God into his affairs, or cite Him as witness.

'Only God can judge me' was a pretty common excuse when we know we were doing something questionable. But how could a just and loving God agree with something that even men would not tolerate? She was still debating with God and lies when the train stopped.

In the city that the masses flocked to and revered, there were promises of eternal life and happiness on every banner. They decorated the front of every church, mosque, and temple along the way to where her temporary home was located.

The cab ride was a series of short jolts, for the roads were filled with pilgrims. The bed and breakfast Jade stayed in was a weathered and aged building in an old quarter of the ancient city.

The medieval door was made of large wooden planks held by iron bands. Spanning the arched top was a cluster of inlaid stylized flowers also in iron. Jade rang the doorbell, a modern feature that looked like it fell from some future and got caught on the wall. The landlady, an older woman in a cream blouse with printed tiny bouquets greeted her. A young man at the front desk checked her in, probably her son, as it was customary in this type of family run establishment.

"Good morning, Miss. I'm Marco, manager. Please sign here and I'll take you to your room. The elevator is this way."

Jade looked at the closet elevator, and claustrophobia's hands reached out for her. She decided to let her suitcase take the lift with Marco while she took the stairs. They met her at the top: "Follow me I'll show you to your room". Jade replied with a thank you and walked behind him. Her room was a few steps past the lift, had a door and a window that opened into the center hall crowned with a skylight. She hoped that was not the only window in the room.

"If you need anything, please let me know" Marco said as he unlocked the door and handed her the keys. Jade nodded, took the keys, then stepped inside. The room was small but very clean, and across from the entrance, there was another door and window open to a large terrace whose privacy was protected by a considerable number of colossal flowerpots. Jade could not help her grin.

Morning was bright behind the tainted glass panes of the elongated windows in the living room.

Not the brightness of diamond, rather the classy shine of pearl. Jade wrapped the cashmere shawl over her shoulders and opened the squeaking front door.

The road was full of maples leaves; they covered the ground, they were still falling from the trees. The red and golden leaves weaved an enchanting tapestry that played its melodious yet secret song with her every step. The moving golden dome let the sky's innocent blue peep through whenever the wind ran amok. Fall was here. Time had passed.

Fall invited running thoughts and far away memories. The ones she cherished and the ones she wished she could forget. Walking by a small building, its serious portico lightened by a bas-relief of angels, and flower boxes along the walls filled with tender colchicum in the colors that soothed the soul. But the gold plaque by the door read 'Varrichio Studio legale' transported her back to bad days at work, when the world was depressing, and the people even more.

Days when she'd gone to work and was met by faces with mouths opened only to criticize and penetrating eyes that saw ugly traits she did not know she had. The physically grown-ups chose to be miserable high-schoolers and tried to drag the world

142

into their misery. One must live one's life the way they did, in inhibition of happiness and arranged freedom of expression. They all went to church.

Personality was unacceptable. How dared people run in the rain to feel the soft touch of Nature on their bare skin? How dared people laugh at jokes and scream in pleasure? How dared people be as audacious as to remain themselves? Those questions might follow these do-gooders day and night like a Zen practitioner's kwan. The quest of truth... They all went to church.

In their magpie colors they looked at the likes of Jade in tropical parrots plumage, wondering what went wrong at birth. The people whom she met at work scared her, because they had the ability to make the world around them filled with sad dreary ugliness. Nobody should laugh too loudly for they might awaken the joy of living the puerile magpies have deeply buried! Not to like one's body because although you are made in the image of God, it was to be feared and shamed instead of loved and respected. They all went to church.

Jade cherished the Sundays and Holidays with her family with the nostalgia of family tradition. The glue that bound them was not faith, but the love for one another. Faith was a personal, intimate, lonely road, Jade had not yet come to the end.

She tried Faith. Hope ran very fast to meet Jade, and as fast, it ran away. She could not let go of reason, her inquisitive mind refused to cohabit with the submission to an unknown higher power, the quantum leap into Religious Faith had never occurred. That Faith had asked her to supply her own answers to questions that dogma could not.

The answer that 'all was planned out' was upsetting when one examined the injustices and uncalled for misfortunes at birth. The divine plan seemed to have too many mysteries. She got tired of being blamed she did not pray hard enough for answers, or pride prevented her from accepting the divine plan, a circular logic that mocked her genuine effort to understand. With that, people who preached compassion were the breathing opposite in their actions. Jade watched them and understood that 'I love My God' simply meant 'I love Myself'. Jade thought they were not after the truth, they were after ratings. And they all went to church.

If salvation is distributed by a divine being, and that salvation is given only on the condition of absolute obedience, then free will is a joke, an aberration of words. When everything revolves around a single deity, it is solipsism.

Jade gave up on metaphysical answers, and focused on concrete, earthly solutions that could help her deal with the present sufferings. She looked for a way of life that could get her closer to happiness, not in an after death realm, but at this present time. People talked about eradicating hunger on a global scale, it was a noble ideal that she admired, but to eradicate anger on a personal scale was her life goal. Anger was bad company. Especially righteous anger. It could kill. She disliked constantly feeling angry at her cheating ex-husband, deceitful ex-best friend, hard to fathom co-workers, and the general unsatisfactory state of life. Jade was ruminating her thoughts when a shout came. "Belle scarpe!" startled her. A car went by the curb, slowly, and the face of a young man with long brown hair smiled at her with another "Belle scarpe!" All the Italian that Jade could mutter was a timid "Grazie" and continued walking. *Nice shoes? Not Nice girl?*

At the intersection Jade consulted her map, then left the old quarter and headed towards Piazza del Duomo. She chose an open space coffee shop in the trendy mall by the plaza to rest and wait for noon time, hoping the perpetual tourists in the city of Dogma would thin out for lunch, or the sacred siesta.

Jade crossed the terrace, heading towards the cathedral. The flow of tourists moving solemnly to the entrance interrupted her pace and her thoughts. Waiting in line for entry, Jade had time to look around. In front of her, in its white magnificent splendor was the marble jewel of a church carved by faith. It did not matter what God they believed in, Faith could create such beautiful art work, or horrendous self-justifying crimes.

Jade's amazement climbed as she ascended the long, stiff and narrow stairways carved in stone to the roof. Her eyes imbued with reluctant tears, moved by the love transpired from every stone block that made the staircases. This, without a shadow of a doubt, was the work of Love. Each stone that paved the path, each stone that formed the walls, were worked to perfection. Exceptional bas-reliefs decorated hidden corners that did not expect visitors' eyes, the secret prayers of the artists to the God they believed in. The forests of spires on the roof reached the sky in such a harmonious way it looked like the manifestation of a melody. She could almost hear the chants and prayers elevated with each spire reaching the sky for salvation.

Jade walked along the wide corridors that bordered the marble roof. The breeze played with her hair, blowing kisses at her cheeks. No noise of the streets could reach this height, this total silence was broken only by the sound of her shoes on the marble. She sat down at a shaded alcove on the East side, away from the inquisitive sun. At the rooftop of the world, on a monument dedicated by love and faith to a God, she was bathed in the peace that faith had erected. It did not matter what that dogma had instructed, the love and faith in it was true and beautiful. The believers found their absolution in the expression of their love. She thought she could live here, in peace, forever.

The shadows of the spires shifted and stretched to remind her time was pressing. Jade left the top of the world bathed in its glorious past for the noisy streets down on Earth. She stopped at each floor along the way down and wandered into several rooms with no windows, used as cells to imprison royal rivals in the battle for the throne. Scratches on the walls had to represent days? Months? Some sort of point of reference for hope, because it had been impossible to guess time inside these foot thick stonewalls. In the most beautiful place dedicated to God, humans found ways to *uglify* it.

As she moved on the uncertain ground of the present, she wondered if people's thirst for security in a slippery future has resulted in the thirst to believe in the existence of an Almighty Being. But Impermanence reigned. This monument too, as dogmas and their followers, would not stand forever in time.

Jade believed there was some order in this vast universe. Since human beings were not the only breath of life in the cosmos, the law that ruled should not leave out other lives. That cosmic order insured the existence of any and all beings.

It seemed God was very different from different perspectives, which to her confirmed that God was the prolongation of Self, of Ego. If God is, let God manifest himself through humans not by their words but by their actions. All her life Jade was told about God by his messengers, who wrote dogmas to solidify an institution, and religious institution is a very lucrative business.

When God fell into the hands of religion, wars broke out. When would human beings take responsibility for their heinous act and stop hiding behind God's intention as an excuse? In this diseased world, she has been trying to find her *raison d'être*.

What she had found was this sad reality: she did not have a reason to live, and she did not have a reason to die.

Jade went to bed wishing her sleep would never end.

What good it is to wake up in the morning and hope is not there to greet me? What good it is to go on, if not to walk with the rising sun into the belief that beauty is here?

The City of Temples

10 Morning rolled back, as loyal as only it could be, and smiled upon her with the twinkling of light dots on her blanket. One foot reached down searching for a slipper, Jade laid half on half off the inviting warm and soft bed.

Further South of this city laid the ruins of another ancient city. The city of Temples. People said sunrise on these Temples was not only breathtaking, it was mystic. But any sunrise in a foreign city would be spectacular for a tourist, since novelty meant beauty, and getting up before the sun did not seem enticing so Jade forwent the alarm and let her natural clock wake her up. She finally got out of bed and started the morning rituals to meet the day. She put on a short sleeve flowing dress and went to the covered terrace used as an open dining room.

"Good morning, Signorina." Diligent Marco was already up and running the inn.

"Buongiorno, Marco."

He put a moka pot in front of her and smiled coyly.

"Enjoy your *mill*, Signorina."

"Grazie, Marco."

There was no bad disposition that a good night sleep and an excellent home cooked breakfast could not repair. And after a shot of café that instantly tamed her indolence, Jade felt up to adventure again. She went down to the front counter, hoping Marco was there. He was.

Jade: "Marco, I'd like to visit the city in the south. What is the best way to do that?"

Marco : "It's best if you have a private driver. Then you won't have to look for a driver each time you go to a different site. There are taxis and tuk-tuks, which are a kind of two-wheel carriage pulled by a motorcycle. Taxis have air-conditioning. Should I call a taxi for you?"

But Jade's heart was already set on the exotic name. Tuk-tuk, for her trip to the south.

* * *

Crossing to the southern zone, to the ruins of what once was a complex of sandstone temples rightly named the City of Temples, Jade expected the sudden change of weather. Here it was either scorching sun or heavy rains.

The tuk-tuk dropped her right in front of the temple. There were people, but not crowded with tourists as in the North. She climbed the steps to a platform connected to a stone bridge. It extended over the large moat that encircled the pinecone roofed temple complex in its protection.

The air seemed alive and the skin tingled with energy. When she looked at the distant structure her heart spun with joy and excitement. And as she approached the temple she felt as if she was going back in time. A peaceful and sacred feel emanated from the edifice, and the closer she got the more ancient it looked. In the company of worn rocks and crumbling walls, she had the feeling that a hundred years were as the blink of an eye.

This temple was not the biggest in size compared to historic monuments in other parts of the world, but the immense feeling of peace dominated all of them. Peace ran with the breeze along the galleries outside the walls, between the pillars, from one tower to another. It slowed her thoughts and the pace of life down to quietude. Visitors wandered and lingered, they did not look curious, but relaxed and rather connected to this place. She saw a young man sitting in the half lotus position at a corner of an inner wall. Motionless except for his breath, he appeared to be part of the architecture and carvings. Jade smiled as she watched him, envious of his discipline.

The voices of other visitors were muffled by the thick sandstone walls, but still distracting, so she went to the end of an obscure hallway to sit down at a corner facing the courtyard, away from the contamination of the crowd.

She thought how the Self was easily swayed, by power or money. The contaminated selves that ran organizations and companies set out to make profit, thus profits dictated the course of their action; the human factor was reduced to a means.

What would happen if money was taken out of politics and religions were taxed? It might eradicate poverty, which is the result of humanity's indifference toward humanity. She felt helpless in her attempt at changing the status quo, for her whole life was chained down by different regulations that claimed they existed for her own good, and by her own abiding to them. Freedom was an illusion.

From the niche where she sat, Jade could see the memories of a bygone temple, reposed in fragments of walls and isolated doorframes.

Dogmas tumbled with time, like the walls of the temple. The doorframe stood alone like a decoration, with no purpose, as useless and beautiful as a rainbow. This side or the other, was there a difference? The fundamental purpose stood with time in its bare truth. The idea of transition. The need to control translated into dogmas and useless principles that translated into control of space with walls, that could not withstand time, the cosmic truth.

She left the main temple to go deeper into the city of ruins. After crossing a burned patch of courtyard lawn, she reached the inner enclosure, the site of another tower. The stairs that led to the entrance were as majestic as the edifice. A man in the hallway holding incense sticks, dashed to the porch to greet Jade when he saw her.

"Incense Miss, burn for the Gods. Good luck for you. Good husband."

Jade looked at the thin man in rags, his faced chiseled by a hard life, eyes shone in hope of a sale and obliged. The exchange made the man's grin grow wider.

There was a giant statue standing by the wall on her left. Light from the open skylight offered a grand scale chiaroscuro of the hall. The face of the deity remained in the shadow while the incense burner at his feet was evident in the oblique sunray. Dragon like smoke dominated the space above the offerings. She burned the stick, but smiled to herself. To whom was she paying respect? *To whom it might concern.*

She walked through the hall to the opposite door and dialed her driver's number. The next complex was about a mile away, and this sun was unforgiving to trekkers.

"Yes, Miss. Sovann here, Miss."

" Sovann, will you pick me up at the back gate, I don't want to walk back to the main gate. Too far."

"The main gate is West, so the back gate is East. The East gate is a long walk from the temple. Nothing to see, forest only. I can pick you up at the North gate. After you leave the temple, turn left, keep going, the North gate is not far".

She was thankful for the driver's tact and care. The walk was not long indeed. She was relieved and happy to see Sovann wave for her from across the street by his tuk-tuk. 'Her' tuk-tuk, a painted crate-on-wheels pulled by a motorbike.

She got off at the beginning of the bridge that led straight to the Stone Smile temple. On both of its sides, gigantic sitting statues held the sacred serpent Naga. Jade was not fond of snakes, but these Nagas looked warm and benevolent, proof that rock had its tender side that only a few stone carvers could reach. From afar she could see the giant face on the tower gate smiling at her. The face was compassionate and strangely calm.

Humidity was palpable. She could feel the change on her skin the minute she crossed the threshold of the gate. She followed the network of dirt roads that led to different towers. They were built several feet above ground level, with intricate carvings that adorned the stone steps in the shape of lotus petals, took visitors to the entrance.

The steps were very high and the doors very low. Jade had to use her hands to hang on to the steps whenever she went up and down. She remembered to watch out for doorways after hitting her forehead several times. Was there a reason or meaning to it, nobody explained, but that feature delighted her.

She followed the steps and found herself in a different plane. Every direction she looked, she saw the calm stone face with its mystic smile.

She saw an immobile figure at one of the multiple doorways on the long wall. The Lady-in-White. The face and the white dress stood out in the shadow. Timeless, beautiful.

They left the arid ground along the inner walls for the greener land further in the depth of the site. There was more life where they were heading. Trees were bigger, higher, and humidity weighed heavier on each breath. The ancient city was once eaten by the forest. Big, strong roots, larger, taller than humans, held captive in their grip what was left of a temple.

"Why am I? Why am I who I am?" Jade asked.

The Lady-in-White did not answer as they walked on the patch of grass, tender green tapestry sprinkled with lavender wild flowers. Lavender, the sun's palette above the temples before saying goodnight. Jade looked at the sky devoid of the bright moving colors it had not long ago. White clouds flew hesitantly in the grayish purple sky. After day, night came. Never failed.

The answered finally came: "You are because Existence is. Existence is born from Love that is the beginning and the end, an infinite circle. You are born from Existence, as the cosmos. Every life carries that love in it, and you are who you are because the spark of life in you chooses to experience life and love this way, as in you create your own fate. Get in touch with that love. The further people drift from that center of love, the worse they get".

Darkness started to spread. It smoothed over the line of reality that outlined the shapes of standalone doorframes, lonely steps, and roofless walls.

The soft voice sounded like a melody of the dark: "Look at the ruins. That's the image of the world. Everything is transient, transient as a dream. Your struggles and joys are not lasting. When you see

158

how you cannot take refuge in impermanence, you know where lies happiness."

Jade whispered: "If everything is impermanent, love, hate, good, bad, then what lasts? What is real in this dream?"

The Lady-in-White said gently: "What is and will always be. Existence, love, the heart, name it however you like. Since birth you have drifted away from home. Find the road home, the road to the heart, is a life lived in essence. To live the essence of existence is to live in love. That should be your religion. The religion of the Heart."

Jade: "You talk about Existence, as in Life. Who creates Life?"

The lady replied: "Can't Existence Be, instead of Being Created? Why does the universe have to have a master? Because human beings run in packs. Like dogs, humans need an alpha superior to lead their life and watch over them."

She added: "Existence is the Existing Love from where all lives sprung".

"Existence is Love? That will leave me with no money," Jade said jokingly.

"Nobody is rich enough to forsake love." The Lady-in-White said as she walked before Jade on the narrow path to an elevated terrace. The hem of her long dress stayed impeccably clean, while Jade's pants started to collect mud of the damp road. As they went up, Jade saw the head, the trunk, then finally the whole elephant guardian of the terrace. There were four elephant statues in four corners, only two won the battle with time and erosion, for the moment.

"I think you're right. People use money to buy love." Jade reprised the conversation. "Money or love is the drive behind many lives."

"Let the appreciation of beauty and the nostalgia of perfection drive you."

They stood in the shade of the elephant statue, at the edge of the terrace, looked down on the ruins at its feet. What's left when dogmas were gone? Beauty? Jade could imagine the horrified expression of her parents, especially her mother, if they could hear these speculations. She did not share their beliefs, but they loved her nonetheless, might be more because they thought she was heading towards infinite sufferings.

She thought about the Lady-in-White's words and concluded that love was inherent to all sentient beings, the natural goodness, before it was clouded by greed, anger, ignorance, and other human attributes.

There were two kinds of religious people. People who were kind because they were religious and people who were intolerant for the same reason. The first kind did not need religion, the second should be expelled for using religion as a cudgel to beat down the masses, *in thy name, O divine will.*

There were children who were born with incurable disease, what kind of just, compassionate, omnipotent God placed that cruel fate on innocent newborns? What God would give one part of his creations a lush land and other part an arid, more naked than dirt, a piece of waste where nothing could grow but sadness and hunger?

"If you hate religion", the Lady-in-White said, "then you are a fanatic non-religious adept. You adopt the same behavior you dismiss as brainless. You compete with religions to claim truth on your side. Truth is not measured by the decibel of your voice. There is a universal truth, let it speak for itself. If you know it, live it".

Jade looked around. Darkness had made its home in the city of Temples. But she could see with clarity with her mind's eyes, that God was in a baby's smile when in his nebulous world he recognized the face of his mother bending over the cradle. God was in the hand that wrote an anonymous check for the neighbor in need. God was in the tears shed on a war so far away from a suburban life that it seemed to happen on a different plane. God was in the last piece of meat that the hungry wife saved for her husband or the moonlight job he took to afford her an easier life. God was in a cure that finally came after long nights of frustration and hard work, in the creation of a new crop that fed a starving population. God was in the caring and sharing the bounty of the earth.

Jade believed in God, but not the bearded despotic God religions made him out to be. God is the silence of true love and compassion. God is the light that leads to the source, to the heart. The inherent humanity buried in each person. And in the freedom each person has to find their own heartbeat and their own God. God is Humanity.

People bought into dogmas to buy themselves a ticket for a heavenly future. But there is no future, only the rolling of infinite present.

The Lady-in-White took her hand as they stumbled their way back to the gate in the encroaching night. Jade could make out under the street light the bright color of her tuk-tuk and Sovann standing by the motorcycle, his head swiveled, looking for his lost client. The other tourists had already left the temple with sunset; the two of them were the lingering sheep.

The Lady-in-White said, "Every erected temple will crumble. Only the temple that has always existed will continue to be. Let the mornings be the roof of your temple, and nights the soft bed. The dealings with people your prayers, and kindness your offerings."

Jade thought: *The temple of life.*

They finally reached the gate. As the driver saw Jade, a big smile relieved his traits.

The Lady-in-White said: "Don't take anybody's truth as yours. Find the fresh fragrance of truth from the engagement of your heart and brain and the temperance of common sense".

Jade looked at her with wondering eyes. *Can't you see that your words resonate with me?*

She concluded: "Remember this, any dogma that is based on fear is control in disguise."

The Abyss of Death

 Jade was asleep and dreamt about a stranger blaring a horn in her ears. She woke up and heard the intercom call passengers out to the hallway that ran in front of all compartments.

The conductor had an important announcement regarding the trip. Jade put on a slipover and went out. People were asking among themselves, "What happened?"

The conductor's voice on the speaker was clear and measured: "First of all, thank you for taking the train, it has been a pleasure serving you on this cruise ship on tracks. Unfortunately, there has been a failure in the brake system due to sabotage. Our crew has done everything possible in their knowledge and ability, but we can't fix it. The emergency brakes were also sabotaged. We are coming down from the mountains and our speed could exceed five hundred kilometers an hour, and the next stop is a small town built on a cliff, Water-Mill of the Sea".

A pause that seemed to stretch beyond patience then the voice came back: "If the train doesn't slow down, it will not make the abrupt turn down along the coast to go into the city. It is possible we could go off the cliff. I'm doing all I can in my ability to control the train and avoid that. Thank you and God bless you all."

Somebody screamed: "This is a joke?"

"This is not true."

"Did he say sabotage? Who did it? Did they catch the bounder?"

Jade and all the other passengers, knew death existed, but they had medicated themselves with living and had pushed such thoughts to the back of their minds. They were enjoying the ride and death was just not on the agenda. As if death would somehow disappear because it was forgotten. But now, the truth long hidden came out like the fire of a struck match in the dark. It did not matter what caused it, death would be waiting at the end of the line.

She had always thought and talked about impermanence and death. But now she was disoriented and fearful. And she could see fear on the faces of the people standing about her, and nothing anyone said helped quiet those fears.

People started moving, some back into their cabins. Jade walked along the corridor that led to the dining car. Everything looked too festive: the flowers, the shining silverware, the impeccable tablecloth swore at the drowning feeling inside her. The fate of the conductor's words sunk in. She could hear crying here and there, muffled behind the compartment doors, lamentations and prayers added to the chaos. Death was closing in on the train, and some people were talking of jumping off the death trap.

Accidental death was looming before them all, but death was no accident. It was scheduled to arrive, it had always arrived, it would always arrive.

The car used as an entertainment room was full. A family whom Jade sometimes said hello to was kneeling on the floor receiving blessings from a priest. Behind them, a queue of alternating calm and distorted faces. A monk in a yellow robe sat in a lotus position in the middle of a circle. The people around him all closed their eyes. Some eyes closed on rather peaceful faces, some on running tears. People prayed standing, kneeling, sobbing.

Suddenly a scream added to the chaos: "He jumped!"

"At this speed, he can't survive!"

A few other men jumped with the direction the train was going. She did not know if they were committing suicide or trying to survive the crash by leaving the train. But she forgot about their fate as soon as that thought brushed her mind. She knew there was no way out alive, and her fear was throbbing.

Overlapping voices of fright, anger, and helplessness now filled the train. Jade fought her way back to her room. Half-way through the smoking lounge that preceded the sleeping car, she felt dizzy and sat down on a bench, where a man sat at the other end calmly extracting pleasure from his cigarette.

"Would you like some water? I can get you a glass." He asked, concern in his voice.

168

Jade shook her head, "I'm fine. Thank you."

"That's the least I can do in this moment. By the way, I'm Kyle."

His even tone induced a note of rationality into the disarray.

Jade fought back her tears: "Jade, nice to meet you."

Jade extended her hand and looked at Kyle. His eyes limpid, his voice normal, it was difficult to detect the fear of death that was consuming her and the rest of the passengers. The bewilderment had to show all over her face, because Kyle said: "I've been diagnosed with brain cancer. So I took this trip. I'm getting used to the thought of dying."

Jade tried to show empathy. To learn about one's death and live the agony until the day it ended sounded worse than their present situation. She would not have to agonize that long.

"I'm sorry", she said.

But Kyle smiled back: "There is no sorrow for learning how to live".

Not knowing how to answer to this, Jade replaced the inadequacy of words with silence.

Kyle asked: "Are you scared?" She knew he saw fear in her eyes. She nodded.

He continued: "My doctors try to show me compassion, my family tries to show love, because this illness is a curse, I am dying too young. Colleagues think I deserve it for offending God, because I'm gay. I feel compassion for them, because I know what they don't know. When I finally accepted what was happening to me, I felt relief and reached a certain level of peace. Since I look at everything as if I'm looking at life from above. What bothers people seems infinitely trivial to me. I live life fuller, and realize I'm lucky, I'm prepared. Death comes to many people as a surprise, I feel compassion for them. They don't have time to work through their fear nor live life intensely like I did."

Jade answered: "There will never be enough time. Fear is everywhere. There is too much suffering. Too much injustice. Too much hate. Too many questions unanswered".

Kyle said in a demure tone: "It's the Why of things, leave it to Because. You will never have all the answers, our time is measured and truth is infinite. Instead, enjoy the spectacle."

Looking out the window, Jade could only see the milky fog covering a small town that they raced passed. Her thoughts also started to fog up when she felt a presence nearby. She turned to look and exhaled in relief when she saw the smile that wiped away all worries and her heart gave a leap of joy. It was the joy of meeting somebody one loved, but did not realize how much one loved them until everything was extracted from life. In the last few minutes, seeing her dear friend was the comfort of returning to a haven without knowing the extent of the need.

The Lady-in-White gave Jade her hand, which she grabbed with gratitude, and led her to the now deserted dining car. The fear of this fatal destination had frozen all the activities of living.

Then the voice which softness reached the soul asked: "Do you want to sit here?"

"Yes." She answered.

They sat at the end of the long dining car, at the table she sometimes took her lonely meals. Jade looked around for a waiter to take her order. Habits died hard.

"We're going to die." Jade said.

"Death is a transition." The lady answered.

"Transition from existence to non-existence?"

"From one form of life to another. You don't need to find eternity anywhere else than in this cycle of life and death. Life in this form ends for another form to begin. A transformation. Water into vapor into rain into water again. You see that happens around you every day. But your own death touches you deeply making you lose sight of reality."

Again, Jade sunk into her thoughts. Could it be that at the end of this journey another adventure might begin, a new life beyond her planning and control, as it was with her birth into this one?

She was taught, implicitly, that wanting and accumulating were good, it's the way to be. The ultimate in being successful was to want and to get what one wanted. Accumulation equaled strength, merit was placed on one's will to triumph over others'. Sometimes the heart was lost in the race, but the success trophy was also the absolution. She remembered running with the pack, hardening her heart to steady the pace. Packed light, no unnecessary emotions, the goal justified the means. Strength was the glorified and ultimate shield against the world. The hero was the heartless winner.

She thought of the fear of losing, in love or in work. But no success could get her over this stage of life. Every milestone with the unforgettable imprint was not so unforgettable anymore. She had blindfolded herself with ignorance, she has been living the shadow of her life.

The Lady-in-White continued: "When you understand that everything that has a beginning will have an end, you will live and die without baggage. You will live and die without resentment. You will live and die without regret. You will live and die free. Because the truth as you perceive is not the Truth. The life you have lived is all perceptions. Your perceptions of forms, which are illusions, they are because you are. It's all phenomena, conditioned to appear and disappear, with or without your attachment to them. Get attached and you're doomed in the constant change of forms."

Jade's fear slowly dissolved in tears running down a calmer visage. Tears of relief.

"What is death if not a breath of life imprisoned in a body finally freed to be one with the cosmic breath; a faint note of life joining the eternal choir. Do you hope that karma, or the law of causes and consequences exists?"

"Yes, I do." Jade nodded.

"Can you make the leap?" The Lady-in-White looked at her, eyes widened with care.

"The leap?" Surprised, she asked.

"Yes. To let Hope mature into Faith. The faith that any good deed will be rewarded. The faith that although you can't take anything with you through the portal of death, karma will follow. The faith that a life lived with compassion or at least with decency will reap a good fate in the continuation of this one. And the opposite is also true. When faith lives in flesh and bone, it is truth".

Jade lowered her voice: "I don't know if I can".

"It is difficult for a small mind to digest an immense truth. And what is the truth cannot be resized to fit into your acceptance. I'm asking you to open to the discomfort of unfamiliar terrain, and dare to fall. Death interrupts the stream of existence, of consciousness, but doesn't end it. Only this numbered lifespan ends. To continue in another form".

The lady's voice seemed to come from her own mind: "Sadness does not come from death itself, but from the nostalgia for the momentary ride that life offers."

A ride that all of us hope will be everlasting, for ourselves and the ones we love.

She walked to a window and leaned her forehead against the glass pane. The meadows along the train tracks became a blurred greenish band under the dark blue strip of sea. The lighter blue of the sky seemed immobile. She turned away and caught a pair of eyes about her waistline staring at her. A wandering child. Jade saw tears on the open face, and wondered if the boy knew what was about to happen.

She asked the boy: "Hi little man. Where are your parents?"

"I don't know. I was sitting with them and I wanted orange juice but my mum was talking to my dad and she didn't hear me, so I went to get orange juice in the kitchen and when I went back I couldn't find them." The answer came in a trembling voice.

Jade felt cold and sat down before her legs gave out. Down on the floor, she was at the kid's height. He might be five years old. She looked at his round face, she looked into his eyes, new and bright, limpid eyes that have not registered images of sufferings in their depth. There was not enough time to look for his parents, the cliff was approaching and the train was in turmoil.

"What's your name, sweetie?" She asked.

"Sky."

"As in Skywalker?"

The kid smiled and nodded, and Jade felt dead inside.

"Do you remember what number is your room?"

" It's 20…, 204. My mom said I am very smart. I can count like big kids".

It was two cars down at the least. He had walked a long way from his parents to look for them. She had to make a decision.

"You are very smart, and very brave. Why don't you stay with me for now, and I'll help you find your parents after… When the grownups go back to their room, it will be easier for your parents to find you too, because there will be no crowd. We'll wait here, deal?"

The boy was on the brink of tears, but nodded.

"Your mom loves you very much." Jade looked into the kid's eyes.

"I know. I want my mum".

Jade moved to a bench, put the kid on her lap and wrapped her arms around him: "We'll see her soon, brave little man. Sleep, or just close your eyes and rest, sweetie. We'll see your parents soon". He acquiesced. Tired from the search for his parents, he closed his eyes.

Jade held the kid tighter. Whatever has form will know decay. But he would never know the sufferings of adults, the falling apart of health. He only knew love and hope, and dreamed of his parents in his last sleep. Jade looked at the boy's round face as he dozed off in her arms. The visage of serenity.

The nebulous quest she chased all her life was answered. This was how she would want it to end. To live life in a way that in her last minutes, she would find serenity.

The journey towards death was a journey towards the sun. The falling into the ocean of no more barriers, or forms, or tomorrow, or expectation, or joy, or sorrow, the complete silencing of struggle, freedom from the duality of every facet of living was liberation. Her thoughts were still running when a big bang threw the train into the vast ocean.

In the darkness they fell. Faces appeared and vanished as she went by. Left behind, the ones she loved, the things she favored; displayed in front of her, the life story she had written. And then she saw the visage of Death. It was her face.

The play unfolded; the performer was also the spectator.

The Awakening

Jade wakes up to the chirping of the birds. Morning has risen on the branches where the early birds are perching. Probably the same ones who live in the trees in her backyard. She fell asleep while relaxing in the crepuscule, the long journey was just one night dream. But Jade does not feel entirely awake nor does this moment in the sunlight seem reality. Slowly display in her mind images of the voyage and her death. She can still smell the magnolias and grass in the city of friends, hear the voice of words in that chateau, see the rotting leafy rug in the clearing where she met the Lady-in-White. She can still feel the humidity in the city of Temples and taste the seawater that flooded the train.

Did I die to live another existence after death, or have I never left this one?

And most of all, she remembers how unhappy she was.

She feels the cramps in her legs, and changes posture. The discomfort sensation reminds Jade she is indeed alive. And happy to be alive. Every pore in her body sings to the ever glorious sun that slowly rises above the trees. Together with the day, she feels a rise of gratitude. She has fared away from all the fears; fear of uncertainty, fear of what-would-people-think, fear of pain, fear of sufferings, fear of being taken advantage; fear of living.

And fear of death, the unknown mystic land. Where does life fit in if the ultimate answer to everything is No More? She feared death as if death is a realm, but death is merely a portal. Fear and preparation for death make it a lasting world.

But Life is not the preamble to death. Life is a pilgrimage to the source of truth.

It's the solitary journey involuntarily taken by each one, on the quest for a happier self. Everyone will arrive. Time holds the seed of happiness. Darkness can't exist where light is, suffering can't thrive where happiness has roots.

180

A bird flies away from the apple tree startles her. She looks up at the tree, covered as much in green leaves as in red apples. No wonder birds prefer it here. Fruits die for these sparrows to live. Life and death in all forms, the beginning beckons the end.

Every duality suddenly breaks its barrier. Nothing is more or less than its opposite. In the pain of separation, she finds the jewel of love. In the madness of the past, she finds today's salvation. In all the wrong choices she has made, she finds the right way out.

Hope has perched on the brink of despair. In all the excessive, ruthless, painful, hurtful ways she has tried to reach that elusive happiness, she finally understands happiness is not a product of the future. For Hope to mature into Faith, she needs to make the leap. If she opens her heart big enough to let in Faith, the belief in the eternal consciousness or the cosmic love that manifests itself in existence, then everyday annoyance will be lost in love, like an insignificant grain of sand lost in the vast ocean of purpose.

The cheaters she has met, the selfish, the racists, the thieves, the crooks she crossed paths with, have tried to find happiness, just like she did, probably in the wrong places, just like she did. For all

181

the pain they may have suffered, just like she has, she can forgive. For her own sanity, she must forgive, because the most terrible of all curses is the inability to forgive. For every bad thing that happened to her, a good thing followed. For every bad person she meets, a wonderful being comes along to keep the balance. Such is the compassion of the cosmos, to ensure existence.

Morning is fully here, enveloped in the warm sunlight. The dream brings to the surface all the significant people in her life that the strain of distance and the pressure of work had eroded their presence.

Pierre. She walked out of his life without explanation, hurried to get married to a guy whom she thought she loved, hurried to get divorced to make up for the previous hasty decision. Then strings of watered down relationships to protect her heart, but that tactic proved to be more hurtful than helpful.

She will write to Pierre, to give him closure, and be honest about her latent feelings for him. The distant but friendly relationship they still have with each other, can it be interpreted as Pierre still cares? Is there a chance? No matter what, it is better to be truthful.

Jade thinks of Yvonne with admiration, how she was and how she is to her. From obscurity to fame, Yvonne stays the same loving friend, her talent and money has not gotten in the way of their friendship, but Jade's own bitter envy has. She found reasons to distance herself from Yvonne.

And Bertha whom she thought gave up on her goal of loosing weight. But Bertha looks and lives happier than Jade does, because she has found a better goal to achieve: inner peace; something Jade could not understand at the time.

About her colleagues and their exuberant love of life. Dissatisfaction with her own life does not give her a better understanding of others', nor do her sufferings bestow on her the right to judge joy and longing for connection. She looks at the world through her profoundly unsatisfied eyes that distort the reason behind other people's acts, and her worries about finances made her angry at the luckier.

About the desire to travel anywhere in the world without restrictions. Point at a place and take off. Even if she could do so, it is chasing the sun. There is nothing poetic about chasing after happiness. An exotic destination is merely a portal to step into happiness. It is not happiness itself. If her state of mind is in a place of infinite beauty, then exploring the parts of that beautiful mind brings a sense of fulfillment that is no different from gazing at the boreal sky, or watching the underwater world of corals, or swimming in the waters of the Aegean Sea, or looking down Tibet from the highest point of the Himalayas.

Instead of living from the beginning, she lives from the end. She's thirty years old, she maybe at one third, or half, or days, from her end. She'll look at things differently from the finish line, sort out the amount of time and attention given to each detail or big dream in her life. Then she can say she lives life to the fullest without lying.

Money means security and freedom, status and respect. As if there is freedom from death. As if status and respect gained from money could ever be equal to respect for the being. Death will knock on her door - if it bothers to knock at all, and the lie she tells herself will end. Security derived from money is a beautiful house built on a hibernating volcano. The lurking eruption has happened to her parents, and the lesson she learned from that was to cling tighter to the security offered by money, an irrational reaction caused by fear. But how much will be enough when there is no cap on the thirst for security?

And let go of control, or the idea that she has any control over the world of phenomenon, to be really free. Then she'll become not careless, but carefree.

Health, and time, the forgotten valuable assets are still available to her.

Her desire to travel, to leave, is in fact the desire to run from her life, from the emptiness inside. Does anyone want to consciously exchange good for bad? Peace for turmoil? If *Right Here* is happiness does one need to go *There*?

A boat that sails away to fulfill its destiny comes home to drop its anchor and enjoys the memories. But if it didn't have a port to dock in, the sea fare is but a wayward journey looking for home.

Wherever she goes, she lugs her problems with her. The new settings will only be temporary distractions. At the end of the day, she'll be one-on-one with unhappiness. And she'll run again searching. She has a house but lives in the homelessness of the mind.

She must learn to die every minute, so that the next will be a new beginning.

With last night, forever gone with time, a day of her life, carrying with it her old self, into the land where yesterday is buried, so that her tomorrow will have today's peace.

The magic of her garden? It's a room in the midst of nature that helps her see what only can be seen in quietude. It's her mandala for happiness, where she is grounded and belongs. In the stillness of her mind, she makes the leap into Self. And touches the ever existing inner peace, her true home.

Soon the music of her peace will break all barriers and transform her surroundings into a land of beauty, for her mind to explore its infinity.

Sunrays become harsher on Jade's face wake her from her reverie. She smiles to the light. *No, no sunspot and freckles, please.* On an impulse, Jade kisses and her forearms, and her hands, the lost and found *Self,* whom makes her prouder of being whole. *I love you, Jade.*

As she walks towards the house, she thinks of her nice neighbor. She must bake a pie for Laurie and give her the recipe. Her late mother's pecan pie recipe that Laurie has asked for but she consciously forgot to share.

Jade shoves the glass door to the side, steps inside to start her favorite weekend breakfast. When she turns around to glide the door back, Jade sees the Lady-in-White of her dream standing by the garden chair, waving, the smile never leaves her face.

Or is she merely an illusion from sitting too long under the sun?

Dear Reader,

Thank you for taking the time to follow Jade on her journey. I hope it was as satisfactory for you reading as it was for Jade living it.

But I don't know if she will keep her promises or not. Will she call Pierre and will she give Laurie the recipe? If you do, I'd love to learn it from you.